HORN

A MATTHEW HARKES THRILLER

TIMOTHY LEWTHWAITE

ISBN 978-0-9897770-0-1 (Paperback Edition)
ISBN 978-0-9897770-1-8 (Kindle Edition)
ISBN 978-0-9897770-2-5 (ePub Edition)

Editing by James Coggins
Book design by Fiona Raven

Printed and bound in USA
First Printing January 2014

Published by Timothy Lewthwaite
Columbia, MD, USA

E-mail: timlewthwaite@hotmail.com

Chapter 1

Damn the rain, Anton thought as he leaned over the steering wheel. The windshield wipers were doing a poor job.

He rolled down the window, desperate for some fresh air and hoping it would make the nausea go away. He wiped the sweat from his forehead, knowing he would have to pull the car over again. Ten minutes earlier, as he had pulled out of Druid Hill Park, a few miles north of Baltimore's Inner Harbor, he had been sick, and he felt the bile rising in his throat again. The sharp taste of his vomit spilled into the back of his mouth, but this time he forced it back down.

He glanced at the two dark trash bags sitting next to him on the passenger seat. He had done it. He could scarcely believe it.

The killing had been easy, so easy. That surprised him. Anton had never killed before, but two months prior they had told him: Blood-In and Blood-Out. He hadn't known then exactly what they had wanted him to do, but he had known he would have to kill. It was common knowledge throughout the neighborhood that Blood-In was the price anyone who wanted to become a full member had to pay. "They" were the Church Street Crew, a gang that controlled ten blocks of blighted East Baltimore neighborhoods. They sold drugs. They ran a prostitution ring. They extorted protection money from local businesses. And they protected their turf with violence. If you wanted to be anybody in the neighborhood, you needed to be a Blood member.

Anton had been selling drugs for them for four years, but he had been a small-time player with neither the contacts nor the credibility to be taken seriously. Eighteen years old now, he had desperately wanted in, so when two Blood members had approached him outside his grandmother's old brick row house, he had agreed to do the job. It was his chance: Blood-In.

His grandmother had seen him talking to them through her front window.

*   *   *

"Anton, you should stay away from those men," she told him when he came into the house. "What did they want?"

"Nothing. They're just friends."

"They're not the kind of friends who will help you."

She was sitting in her faded armchair, looking out at the world through the anonymity that her living room window provided. She rarely left the house these days, only coming out to sit on her front stoop when the summer heat made staying inside unbearable.

"The neighborhood has changed," she said in a low voice, and Anton couldn't tell if she was speaking to him or herself. "It's not a community anymore. All the old people are gone, moved away or died. I don't know these new people on the street."

Anton looked at her as if seeing her for the first time. She was old and frail. Her husband had been a good man,

but when he had passed away, all he had left her was this
rat-infested house with poor plumbing and a leaky roof in
a neighborhood that stunk of trash when the city garbage
trucks didn't come. Anton knew he should be grateful to
her. She had done her best to raise him after his mother
had gone. He only had a vague memory of his mother. She
had wasted away in this very house, in her tiny bedroom
with the sagging ceiling, the mildew stains on the walls
and the dirty, cracked window that hadn't been cleaned
in years. It had been a bad place for anyone to die. Anton
wasn't sure whether the AIDS had led to the drugs, or her
addiction to the drugs had caused the AIDS. His grandmother had protected him from the worst of his mother's
last months, but in truth, he had been too young to fully
understand what was going on. Her death had left him
hollow and angry.

As he looked around the room, with his grandmother
sitting in her faded armchair and the old paint peeling
from the walls, he knew he had to make a change. The
house was dying.

She looked at him for a moment, but he couldn't read
her eyes. Like her chair, they were fading and sunken.

"Could you get me a cup of coffee and my cigarettes
before you go out?" she asked.

*   *   *

He was now driving south on Route 83 toward the
Inner Harbor. Two police cars sped north as he passed by
the massive Central Booking facility. He had been a young
boy when it was being built, but in its short existence it
had developed a fearsome reputation. Crowded and dirty

holding cells were the least of it. Stories of prisoners going in to be processed but coming out dead were regularly passed around the neighborhood. Everyone knew someone who had been killed, and too many of the stories involved that building. Anton didn't know if they were true or not, but still the building reminded him of what was at stake, of what would happen should he be pulled over. He knew Central Booking would be the least of his worries. In his mind, he retraced what he had done.

* * *

Shooting the veterinarian was simple. He waited until she turned away from him to unlock the rhino's enclosure, pulled a pistol out of his sports bag and shot her in the back of the head. She was dead before she hit the ground. The tranquilizer gun in her hand clattered to the ground next to her. He had wondered whether he would be able to pull the trigger, but it proved remarkably easy when the time came. He had only met her earlier that evening. She was a middle-aged woman, not unattractive, with shoulder-length brown hair and brown eyes, but it was clear the years had taken a toll. He had been told that she had agreed to get him into the enclosure and sedate the rhino. She was the only one who didn't know she would die that night. He had picked her up at midnight in a small neighborhood near Fells Point, not far from Johns Hopkins Hospital. They hadn't talked much as they had driven to the zoo. Her death, simple as it was, was the first part of his Blood-In price.

Killing the rhino, however, was not going to be so easy. He put the pistol away and took the shotgun out of the bag. They had told him where to aim to kill it quickly, but his first shot caught the animal in the shoulder and only wounded it. Frightened at the sound of the gun and enraged at the pain, the animal charged about its enclosure, trying to find an escape. Anton panicked at the sight of the wounded animal. He hadn't expected it to be so big and fast, and shooting through the heavy steel bars that protected the keepers when they worked with the rhino was more difficult than he had anticipated. He kept shooting, each shot thudding into the animal, tearing muscle and flesh, but not killing it. It was too big to miss, but it was moving too quickly for Anton's increasingly erratic aim to produce a kill shot. Then, suddenly, it was on him. The animal slammed into the bars where Anton was standing. He staggered back, pulling the shotgun back through the bars just in time to save the barrel from being crushed by the weight of the frightened rhino against the cold, unyielding steel. As the animal started to stumble away, stunned by the impact and starting to feel the loss of blood, Anton pushed the barrel of the gun back through the bars and aimed just behind the rhino's shoulder. This time he got it right. The shot shattered the rhino's ribs, ripping through muscle and fat before tearing its heart to pieces. The great animal staggered for one step before its legs gave out and it slumped to the ground, lying still in a puddle of its own urine and blood.

It died as he stepped over the body of the dead vet and entered the enclosure. A deep, final breath rasped from its shattered lungs as its eyes glazed over.

Fuck the gun, he thought. *That rhino just wouldn't go down. Why did they give me a shotgun like that to kill a rhino?*

Walking up to the inert rhino, Anton put the barrel to

HORN

the side of the animal's head and pulled the trigger one final time. He was no hunter, and the size of the animal frightened him. Despite what his eyes told him, he wanted to make sure it stayed down.

He stopped for a moment and listened. There was no sound—the rest of the zoo was still asleep. The walls of the rhino's enclosure had muffled the sound of the gunshots. He glanced at his watch. He still had four or five hours before the zoo's morning routine would start, but he didn't want to waste any time, not now, so close to finishing the job. The Blood-In price was now paid. All he had to do was deliver the two packages and he would be a full member. He put the shotgun back in the sports bag.

Blood coated the floor as he knelt down, reached into his bag, pulled out a saw and began to cut at the base of the great horn. His arm was aching by the time he was able to cut through and pull the horn away from the head.

"What do they want with this?" he said as he pulled out a black trash bag and placed the horn inside.

He then started on the smaller horn. After he had cut that as well, he stood up, looked at the devastated animal lying prone in front of him and felt nothing. He picked up the bag with the guns and saw, turned and walked back to the dead vet. She lay face down in an expanding pool of blood. It seemed like an eternity since he had shot her, but only a short time had passed. This would be different from cutting the rhino, he knew. He knelt down, brushed the hair away from the back of her neck and took out the saw again.

* * *

Thinking about it brought back the nausea, and this time he wasn't able to hold it. Jerking the wheel, he pulled over to the curb, opened the door and vomited onto the pavement. Blood-In, he told himself.

As he cleared the Central Booking building, the sound of the sirens and the reflection of the flashing lights faded as he put more distance between himself and the two police cars. Traffic was light at this time of morning, but he was driving a nondescript little blue Ford the Crew had supplied him with, and it blended in well enough. The rain had almost stopped as he turned right on East Lombard Street and drove through downtown Baltimore. The plan was to drive through the city, within a couple of blocks of the Baltimore City Police headquarters, head out to Route 95 and take that south towards the small town of Laurel.

Despite feeling sick and wanting to get away from the area, Anton kept his speed low and made sure to stop at all the red traffic lights. It only took a few minutes before he was able to turn left past Camden Yards and the Ravens' stadium and begin heading out of the city. He wasn't sure whether it was the fresh air or the fact that he was leaving Baltimore behind him, but he started to feel better. He spent much of the drive checking his rearview mirror to make sure nobody was following. He knew that once he was through Baltimore, the chance of the police catching him dropped, but that didn't stop him looking.

Laurel was a small town halfway between Baltimore and Washington, DC. It had been founded in the 1800s as a cotton mill town on the banks of the Patuxent River, but now it was better known for horse racing at Laurel Park. None of this was of interest to Anton as he drove into the town twenty minutes later. He didn't know anything about Laurel, apart from where he was going. He didn't really know much about the world outside of the few blocks of East Baltimore that had been his home.

The drive down Route 95 had been quiet. He had driven the route from Druid Hill Park to the three-level townhome several times in the previous week to make sure he knew where he was going, at first during the day and then at night.

During those earlier visits, the house itself had been empty except for a table in the living room and a couple of chairs. As he pulled into the driveway, he noticed the second floor lights were on. He hit the automatic garage door opener and drove the car inside. The neighborhood was still quiet, and he was certain that no one had noticed the car going into the garage. He turned the engine off and shut the garage door behind him.

As he was getting out of the car, the door at the end of the garage opened. It was Small. He was one of the two original Crew members who had recruited Anton to do the job. He was big, at least six-foot-three, muscled and lean. He had been an all-state linebacker at school before he had blown his knee out in his senior year. Anton had heard the story when Small had shown him how to use the pistol and the shotgun in an abandoned warehouse. Despite his growing familiarity with Small, the man worried Anton. There was something detached about the way he dealt with people, a certain emptiness. Small, Anton had decided, was not a man he would get on the wrong side of.

"You got the two packages?" Small asked from the doorway.

"Yeah, I got them right here."

"Leave the guns in the car and bring the packages upstairs," Small said and then turned and went back into the house.

The two trash bags were surprisingly heavy and awkward as Anton carried them up the stairs to the second level of the townhouse. As he walked into the living room, he saw that two well-dressed Asian men were sitting in the chairs on the other side of the table. They weren't Chinese or Korean, he thought, as he'd seen plenty of them in East Baltimore at one time or another. Beyond that, he had no idea where they could be from. They were both in business suits, and one was smoking a cigarette. Anton wondered what they could possibly want with the rhino's horns and the head of the dead zoo veterinarian. But he knew he wasn't there to ask questions. He had paid his Blood-In price earlier that night, and now he was just there to deliver the contents of the two trash bags. Whatever they wanted with the head and the horn was their business.

Small was in the kitchen to his left as he stepped into the living room. He nodded to the two men.

"What's up?" Anton said to ease the tension.

"Show them the packages," Small said, still in the kitchen. Neither of the other two men said a word.

Anton walked forward, put the two trash bags onto the table and stepped back.

The two Asian men stared at him for a moment. Then one of them leaned forward and looked into the bag that contained the head of the vet. He paused and stared at its contents for a moment but didn't react—no emotion, no distaste. That annoyed Anton. The whole thing had made him feel sick. The killing had been easy, but sawing off the head and driving it to Laurel had been different. He wasn't angry with the man, just his own weakness, his own inability to detach himself from the gruesome nature of the butchery. That was something he'd have to work on.

The man smoking the cigarette had not bothered to look into the bag; his gaze remained on Anton. His partner opened the second bag, and a faint smile played across his face.

Damn, Anton thought. *It's just a piece of a dead animal.*

It was almost imperceptible, but Anton noticed it: the mildest of nods from the man with the cigarette.

Small moved with incredible speed and agility for a big man. Anton was about to say something when Small's strong hand wrapped around his forehead and pulled his head back. The knife was so sharp that Anton hardly felt it cut as Small sliced it deeply across his throat. Blood splashed into Anton's mouth and poured down his neck as he collapsed to his knees. The last words he heard as he pitched forward were "Blood-Out."

Chapter 2

"This is going to be a bad day," Natalie said as she sat behind her desk. "The news of the dead rhino and an executed vet will send shock waves through the entire zoo community."

"It's already international news, and my guess is the story is only going to grow," Matt Harkes answered. "A few years ago, a tiger was poached at a zoo in India, but in America? There are going to be a lot of questions coming our way very quickly."

Natalie gave a weak smile. "Sharon in PR is already lining up media interviews for me. We'll be doing a press conference later this morning. I'll also need to reach out to the folks in Baltimore."

Matt studied the woman across the desk from him. Natalie Harmon was a middle-aged woman of average height with brown hair, green eyes and a plain face. She lacked Matt's own commanding presence—tall and handsome with piercing blue eyes and short, thick, black hair—but he did not for a moment underestimate her power. Natalie was the director of the National Zoo in Washington, DC, and she had recruited Matt ten years earlier. They had met at an industry conference where Matt had presented a paper on Atlantic titi monkeys. At the time, she had been curator of the National Zoo's Amazonia exhibit, but even then he could tell she had her sights set on bigger things. Over the years, he had become a trusted lieutenant, and his career had progressed in sync with hers. Matt was now the curator of large mammals, and the zoo's three white rhinos were under his care.

"The first thing we need to do is call an emergency meeting of the senior staff," Natalie continued. "If this could happen in Baltimore, it is not too far-fetched to think it could happen here."

"We should also coordinate with Jim Reed in Saint Louis since he's the chair of the Rhino Specialist Group," Matt said. "He's got the national profile and the expertise to talk about the impact this will have on the zoo industry's rhino conservation efforts."

"Good idea," Natalie said. "I'll give him a call before I talk to Baltimore and get everyone on the same page with the media. You're an advisor to the Rhino Group. Just how important was the Baltimore rhino?"

"It was an incredibly important animal, I'm afraid. It was just recently imported from Namibia as a new founder for the black rhino population in North America. It took several years to get the Namibians to agree to send it over, and it wasn't cheap—three million dollars, plus a million a year in leasing fees. More importantly, it was a new bloodline that we might not now be able to replace."

Natalie leaned back in her chair. "Poaching in Africa, Asia and Latin America has always been a problem. But killing a vet and slaughtering a rhino in a zoo in the middle of a major east coast city—this really is a chilling development."

"It really is," Matt agreed.

"You're scheduled for your vacation later this week, aren't you?" Natalie asked.

"Yes, but don't worry. I'm staying in Maryland. I'll be going deer hunting for a few days."

"When you go, just make sure to keep your phone with you."

*　*　*

Three days later, Matt was up a tree in his deer stand when his cell phone vibrated in his pocket. The previous three days had passed in a blur, as the staff at the National Zoo had beefed up security arrangements—a daunting challenge with 2,000 animals spread over 163 acres. However, when no new reports of attacks on animals at other zoos had come in, Natalie had relaxed somewhat. The staff had returned to their normal routine, and Matt had been released to start his holidays.

It was mid November, and the rain earlier in the week had given way to a light snow. A wet summer in Maryland had led to a spectacular fall. Bright reds, yellows and oranges had painted the trees for several weeks, but that had passed, and winter was looming. The now fallen leaves were covered with a dusting of white. This particular grove of trees was one of Matt's favorite areas. It was in a gentle valley that provided shelter for white-tailed deer and was next to a stream-watered field that offered good grazing.

He loved the quiet, the stillness, of the woods. It was a trait he had picked up from his father. When he had been a boy, his father would take him duck hunting on the Eastern Shore, close to Chesapeake Bay. They would sit for hours in the blind waiting for waterfowl to fly in, their golden retriever, General, always ready for the signal to leap into the water to retrieve a bird. Matt fondly remembered the first time he had brought a duck down. His dad had let him give General the sign to fetch the duck. He had refrained for a moment, letting the anticipation in General build, and then, with a simple hand sign, he had released the dog. The pent-up energy had exploded in a huge splash as General had plunged into the water. It was a moment that made Matt smile to this day.

They had returned home for his mother to clean the duck and his dad to roast it over a small fire pit outside the farmhouse they called home. The fat had dripped and crackled in the fire, and the smell of roasted meat had mingled with the fresh air. As he thought back on it, Matt knew that night had marked a deeply meaningful rite of passage. It was when he had become a hunter, just like his father.

Over the summer, he had visited this area on his days off to set up his tree stand. He had been hunting then as well, but only with his camera. The Maryland Department of Natural Resources surveyed the area each year to determine a quota of deer to be culled. Matt liked to do his research, and it provided a way to extend his season beyond the fall. He would photograph the deer frequenting the area to study the population. Over the years, he had built up an extensive visual database of the area's white-tailed deer, and he liked to keep it up to date. He would get his hunting friends together at the start of the hunting season and share the information.

The buck he was after this particular day was a spectacular animal with twelve points on almost perfectly symmetrical antlers. When he had first encountered it, it had been a young animal just entering its prime. Those first years, it had appeared both summer and fall, but recently it had only presented itself in the summer. Matt knew that it was the dominant breeding buck in the area and for several seasons had passed its genes on to the next generation. It would soon be beyond its prime, and Matt knew it was time for it to be culled.

He reached into his pocket and pulled out his cell phone. It was a useful piece of technology, he admitted, but he resented the intrusion it could cause in his life. He looked at the touch screen. It was not the call he had expected. He rested his shotgun on his lap and hesitated for a moment before answering, not sure he wanted to talk to her. However long the conversation took and in whatever direction it went, Matt knew he'd be distracted for some time to come.

"Suzanne, how are you?...What's that?...Yes, I'm fine. Actually, I'm up a tree at the moment."

Suzanne Winfield. Deep brown eyes flecked with gold when the light hit them the right way and long, black hair that spoke to her mother's Italian lineage. He could picture her as she spoke.

Matt had fallen in love with her at first sight. It had proved to be a blessing and a curse. They had met at a reception following a presentation by a National Geographic photographer. They had found they shared an interest in the developing world, and a deep friendship had blossomed. Then she had left Maryland for a fellowship at Harvard University, and Matt had continued his studies in conservation biology. A few months later, Matt had traveled north to attend her wedding. In the fifteen years since, and through her two divorces, they had remained close friends.

"How are the deer faring?" Suzanne asked, and Matt could sense her smiling through the phone.

"I'm sure they will be touched by your concern," Matt said.

It was an easy conversation, and they found themselves laughing at shared memories. Matt knew she had called for a reason but decided to let her come to it in her own time.

"Well, I think I can end my hunt. There won't be a deer within miles of me now."

"Are you going to be in town at Christmas?" she asked. "I'd love to see you. I've got something I'd like to talk to you about."

"I should be around," he said.

"Wonderful! I'll tell my parents you'll be coming."

They said their goodbyes, and Matt put the phone back in his pocket. He leaned back in the tree stand, took a deep breath of the cool, fall air and smiled. He unloaded his shotgun and lowered it to the ground before climbing down from the stand. A few flurries of snow blew by in the wind, and he knew he was lucky to be here.

Deep in thought, Matt found himself coming out of the woods and walking up the hill to the farm where he was parked. He climbed through a fence into one of the pastures. A herd of six horses stood rigid, staring at him, with their ears pricked and their nostrils blowing out powerful bursts of steam. Matt knew they were assessing him. Suddenly, they galloped to the far end of the field, where they stopped and stared at him again. Matt marveled at how, after generations of domestication, they still held onto their wild heritage. His thoughts locked on to the rhino slaughtered the previous week and how there had been nowhere for it to run.

As Matt packed his equipment into the back of his black Jeep, he felt his phone vibrate again.

"Can you come in to work tomorrow?" Natalie asked. "Sorry to break up your vacation like this, but I wouldn't ask if it weren't important."

"Sure can," Matt said. "Is this about the rhinos?"

"Yes, that and the budget. I've got a meeting with Steven Reddman, and I'd like you to be there. He's the president and CEO of Genesis Incorporated."

"Yes, I know who he is. I saw a presentation of his a couple of years ago at that conference in Houston," Matt said. "He's been pushing the idea of frozen zoos as a way to maintain genetic diversity in captive populations."

"That's right," Natalie said. "Ever since he resigned as zoo director in San Diego, he's been raising venture capital and building a business model to put frozen zoos on a sustainable financial footing."

"What's our angle with him?" Matt asked.

"Well, you know about the budget issues the zoo is facing—we've got to cut fifteen percent, and that is going to hurt in a lot of ways. What you don't know is that the Under Secretary of Science at the Smithsonian has charged me with growing revenue."

"That's a difficult thing to do when you are cutting that much from the budget," Matt said.

"Yes, it is. The phrase the Under Secretary used was 'non-traditional revenue enhancement.' What he meant was, 'Get more money.' I am looking to float the idea of Reddman leasing the zoo's Conservation Biology Institute in Front Royal. I can't sell it now with property values as depressed as they are, but leasing it will provide a steady income and put our people at the center of any new conservation initiatives Genesis develops."

"You're going to let him lease all 3,200 acres?"

"Yes. Reddman and Genesis are looking for a new head-quarters with easy access to Capitol Hill."

"Wouldn't that mean handing over to Genesis all of the zoo's research and conservation programs, including our own frozen zoo? I thought you were opposed to putting such vast quantities of genetic material from endangered species into private hands?"

"I was, but I don't see any other options. A financially stable, privately run frozen zoo would bring costs down, and breeding recommendations could be more easily made and tracked. You knew Reddman acquired the San Diego Zoological Park's frozen zoo, but that was just the beginning. He's now made similar arrangements with several other facilities. Cooperation between zoos and the private sector is inevitable. There's no other way forward." Natalie paused. "And you may need to pack your bags. Reddman is looking for someone to go to Namibia to do a preliminary assessment on collecting genetic materials from the black rhinos in Damaraland."

"And you've put my name forward?" Matt asked.

"That's right," Natalie replied.

"I'll see you at 8:30 a.m.," Matt said.

* * *

Matt was on time for the meeting the next morning, but he sensed Natalie and Reddman had been talking for some time when he walked into the office. Reddman was large, in his mid to late sixties, with a deep, weathered tan from a life spent outdoors. Cropped gray hair spoke of a military background. He was tall, over six feet, and Matt could tell the years were starting to wear on him. Sharp blue eyes, however, spoke of a deep intelligence that had stood the test of time.

Reddman stood up to shake Matt's hand and held it firmly, locking his eyes on Matt's. There was a challenge there. It quickly vanished. *A silly game*, Matt thought.

After some small talk, Natalie and Reddman quickly got around to the idea of sending Matt to Namibia.

"I need a conservation expert with the people skills to soothe frayed relationships with the Namibians," Reddman said. "I also need somebody with extensive field experience."

"Have you considered sending Jim Reed from the Missouri Zoo?" Matt asked.

"Of course, but with the media circus surrounding the Baltimore incident, his profile is too high. I want things done quietly." Reddman paused and then continued. "We need to make nice with SWAPO on this. They aren't happy about the Baltimore rhino at all, and they are the ones with the real pull. Plus, Jonathan Tuhadeli—he'll be your main contact when you get over there—has some concerns about the police. There's been poaching in the region, and he tells me it may be an inside job. If you find that genetic collection is feasible, then I will contact the Ministry and bring in the Namibians. For the time being, I'd like to keep this off their radar. Tuhadeli is on board with that."

"SWAPO is the South West Africa People's Organization and is the ruling political party in Namibia," Natalie interjected.

The idea of going to Namibia appealed to Matt on a number of levels. He understood the challenges facing the black rhino population, both in North America and in Africa. Time was running out for both. A bold new initiative was needed, a new way of thinking about how the species could be saved. Matt wasn't entirely convinced that Reddman's frozen zoo strategy would work, but he was even less convinced that the more conservative models currently being used would succeed in the long run.

"The days of being able to collect wild specimens are going fast," Reddman explained somewhat wistfully. "Wild caught animals are always highly valued as new bloodlines in collections."

Reddman paused and looked hard at the other two. "I've been in this game a long time," he said at last. "I remember when bringing in animals from the wild was a regular practice and sustainability of populations was not a major concern. The animals were on exhibit to entertain. But, as people have grown more knowledgeable, zoos have had to evolve. Developing countries are getting far more sophisticated too. They are really starting to understand the value of all their assets, wildlife included. The death of the Baltimore rhino will make any transaction with them far more difficult. And the insurance rates are going to go through the roof on any live animal that we want to transport into the country."

"That's where the frozen zoos come in?" Matt asked.

"Yes, precisely. If we don't develop a model to replenish bloodlines, across all species, not just rhinos, we are going to lose almost all of them within the next century. You know the challenges the black rhino population faces in North America. Wild populations are just under too much pressure. If we don't do something now to preserve the genetic material currently in the wild and use it to save the species in zoos, we face losing both. That's why Namibia is so important."

"The Damaraland rhinos are a test case, then, to see if a model can be developed to collect genetic materials from a wild population?"

"Collect it, yes, but on a larger scale than people are currently considering. We need to sample a complete cross section of the population. Imagine a centralized genetic bank of black rhinos. Think of the power of a tool like that—to be able to ensure the viability of the captive population. And if the wild population goes extinct, we can maintain a healthy population for future reintroduction. The Damaraland rhinos are the last free-ranging population of black rhinos in Africa. They are a widely recognized and much loved animal, even more so now, after Baltimore. If we can prove this can be done, then people will start to buy into the vision."

Matt leaned back in his chair and thought for a moment. "To do something like this is going to be incredibly expensive and difficult," he said. "We'll have to develop protocols for everything—sedation, transportation, temporarily housing them, giving them physicals, collecting the materials and releasing them back to their habitat, not to mention ensuring the long-term viability of the frozen samples."

"You're right on all counts," Reddman said. "I've spent the last fifteen years developing a business model for this, and people have scorned me. But why shouldn't innovative business practices be applied to conserving the world's wildlife? Over the last ten years, I've raised venture capital and, as you know, acquired the assets of a number of frozen zoos to build the infrastructure needed. Now it is time to put those assets to work—and the first phase is Damaraland."

Matt looked at Natalie. She'd been largely quiet through the conversation. "What do you think?"

"I think we are at a crossroads. If we don't do something dramatic, there will be no zoos in a few decades. There won't be any animals to exhibit, at least not any of the charismatic and endangered species we have today. The expanded, centralized frozen zoo model holds out some hope. It would be great if we could come together as an industry and do this, but the money just isn't there, nor is there a real consensus. Too many egos, and everyone is cutting back, including us, and we are doing it when the situation demands we expand our efforts. A successful operation in Damaraland may be the best way to make people rethink how we go about conserving endangered species and preserving captive populations."

"Well, the first thing we'll need to do is carry out a preliminary assessment of the area. We'll have to find out how many rhinos there are and how easy they are to track. Then we'll have to get an idea of what infrastructure and facilities are already available and an idea of those that aren't," Matt said. "I can be ready to travel in a few days."

Chapter 3

The flight from New York to Hosea Kutako Airport in Windhoek was as brutal a trip as Matt could remember. He then rented a car and drove north on the B1 to the commercial town of Otjiwarongo, where he booked into a small lodge a couple of blocks off the main road. He had arranged to meet Jonathan Tuhadeli the next morning in the town's central shopping district, but for now all he wanted was sleep.

When morning came, he was still feeling jet-lagged but knew it was time to get to work. Most of the houses on the walk to the café were hidden behind tall security walls, some topped with razor wire. He passed a couple of day laborers sitting against one of the walls. "Hello," he said and smiled as he walked by. The two of them smiled back and nodded, but didn't say anything.

The café was on the bottom floor of a drab, two-story building. There were three small round tables with simple metal chairs around them. The interior was painted a light blue, but looked like it could use a fresh coat of paint.

"Móre meneer," a middle-aged woman behind the counter greeted him. "Hoe can ek u help?"

"Coffee, please," Matt replied. He didn't speak Afri-kaans, but her meaning was clear.

She looked him over briefly, then, apparently approving, went back into the kitchen. She came back with a small pot of black coffee.

"English?" she asked as she put the coffee on the table.

"No, American. I just got into town."

"Are you going to Etosha?" she asked, her command of English surprising Matt. Otjiwarongo was a regular way station for tourists traveling from Windhoek to see the country's signature national park.

"Actually, no. I am here to look for wildlife though. I'm headed to Damaraland for the rhinos."

"That was a terrible thing that happened in your coun-try to our rhino. It has been in the news ever since. Have you seen today's paper?" she asked.

"No. Why? Is there something new?"

"The front-page story has been about that for two weeks now. They write about nothing else, but today there is something new. It says the guns used to kill the woman and the animal were South African guns, guns used by the South African army. Can you believe that, hey? And the lady, the one who was killed, her head was cut off after she had been shot. Who would do such a thing? Kill a woman and then cut her head off. Animals, I tell you, they must have been animals."

Matt was stunned. Despite the intense coverage, there had been no mention of either of those facts in the Ameri-can press.

"Anika, could you get today's *Namibian Star*, please," the lady called out to the kitchen. She turned back to Matt and continued in a quieter tone. "It seems a strange thing to go to America to kill a rhinoceros, doesn't it? Here, yes, they are killed. God forgive us for what we do to his creatures, but to kill a rhino in America, that is a very strange thing, don't you think?"

Matt nodded in agreement. In truth, he had been thinking about the Baltimore rhino a great deal, and it didn't make sense to him. Rhino horn was worth its weight in gold, worth more than gold in fact, but there were easier places to poach rhino than at a North American zoo. The risks were immense. Whoever had planned it must have known a media firestorm would ensue, and, with that, intense scrutiny from some of the best minds in criminal investigation in America.

"Móre meneer, the paper," a young voice said.

Matt looked up and saw two kind blue eyes looking at him, only briefly; then they glanced down. They belonged to a pretty face, a face framed by hair pulled back in a single braided ponytail. Matt guessed Anika was eighteen or nineteen.

Matt took the newspaper she offered and smiled at Anika and her mother. "How do you say 'thank you' in Afrikaans? You are both being very kind to me this morning."

"Dankie." The mother smiled and blushed a little. "Anika, go and get the piesangbrood for our American friend. I think you call it banana bread in your country. You should not drink coffee and read the newspaper without something to eat."

The newspaper story laid it all out in gruesome detail. A pistol and a shotgun had been found next to the burnt-out remains of an old car in an abandoned lot near Sparrow's Point Steel Yard. Ballistics showed that the pistol, a South African military model, had been used to kill the vet at the zoo. The shotgun was also a South African military model, but the serial numbers had been removed from both guns. Even more disturbing, another body had been found near the car, a body covered in blood that had come from both the dead vet and the Baltimore rhino. The body was of a young African-American male, and it, too, was missing its head. There was no sign of the rhino horn or either of the two missing heads.

Just then, a large African opened the door and walked over to Matt.

"Matthew Harkes?" the man asked in a deep, friendly voice and offered him his hand.

"That's right. Jonathan Tuhadeli, I take it?"

"Yes," Tuhadeli said sitting down. "Good to meet you. A coffee for me as well, thank you."

The lady frowned and walked into the kitchen, coming back out a few moments later with a cup of black coffee that she put on the table in front of Tuhadeli without speaking. She turned quickly away and walked back into the kitchen with her daughter in tow, leaving Matt and Tuhadeli alone.

Tuhadeli watched her go and then turned back to Matt. "I am afraid the mistrust between Afrikaners and we black Namibians runs deep," he said as he put some cream in his coffee. "Whenever I visit a town, I try to visit an Afrikaner establishment, but the reaction is mostly the same. Perhaps one day, with all my visits, it will change, and one day we might be able to sit under a marula tree and share a friendly conversation."

"But not today?"

"No, my friend, not today. But it is early yet. We are a young country with a troubled past." Tuhadeli flashed a smile. "It was not so long ago that we were killing each other, you know. So, to have a cup of coffee, even served with a hard face, is progress. But you are not interested in our history, are you? You are here for the rhinos."

"That's right. But reading this makes me wonder if there is a connection," Matt said as he put the newspaper on the table. "South African guns used to kill the vet and slaughter the rhino in America. That is strange. Why choose South African military guns?"

"I read that this morning, and I do not know about the guns," said Tuhadeli. "It is bad news. Much of Namibia is prospering now. Peace and stability have finally come to the country. With the ANC firmly entrenched to the south, Angola emerging from years of warfare to the north and a prosperous and stable Botswana to the east, we are starting to see some signs of economic growth. But it is a fragile growth, and stories like this can be damaging."

"So, you are interested in the betterment of your people?" Matt asked.

"Let me ask you a question, Matthew," Tuhadeli said. "In America, what state are you from?"

"Maryland."

"But you consider yourself first an American?"

"That's right," Matt answered.

"You see, I am a Namibian, but I am from Damaraland. My people, the Damara people, come first, and then I am a Namibian. It's an important difference between you and me. As you travel into my homeland, you will see it is a beautiful country, but it is harsh. Many people still struggle each day to make a living from the land. It is those people, my people, who I work to help."

"And what's your interest in the rhinos?" Matt asked.

"Did you know that every rhino is owned by the

government of Namibia? They are a national resource, much like the diamonds to the south or the uranium mines near Swakopmund. Only they are in Damaraland, where there are no diamonds or uranium. They are a means to an end, a way to improve the lot of my people."

"What about the poaching in the area?" Matt asked.

"There is poaching of the rhinos, but who is doing the poaching I have not been able to figure out. I worry that the police may be involved."

"And how can you help me access the rhinos?" Matt asked.

"We must first go to Khorixas. It is a small town where I am based, but it has the supplies you will need to explore the wilderness. I have a vehicle for you and a guide who can help you search for the rhinos. But we must do this quietly as many powerful people are not happy with the death of the rhino in Baltimore. If they hear there is an American in the country looking to assess the black rhino population so quickly after what happened in your country, there will be many questions—questions we are not yet ready to answer."

* * *

The vultures circled slowly and dropped towards the ground. Matt knew that when they gathered in large numbers like this, it meant one thing: death, death on a large scale.

On his second day at work in Damaraland, Matt was surveying the area south of the dry Hoanib River, looking for signs of black rhino. He had yet to see any, but he would have three weeks in Namibia. The first night they had returned to Khorixas to sleep, but his plan for today was to establish a base camp and get a better feel for the land and the wildlife. To harvest genetic material from a wild population of black rhino would be complicated and expensive, but when Reddman and Natalie had brought the idea up, Matt had been enthusiastic. He had recognized the potential value a large collection of viable material would have for sustaining rhinos, and the techniques used could be applied to other species.

The land was harsh and barren, a rocky desert with a few stands of mopane trees clinging hard to the scorched banks of seasonal rivers whose sandy beds had been dry for months. Matt took out his canteen and took a mouthful of water. The water had been cool when he had left Khorixas early in the morning, but it was now hot. It was early afternoon, and the sun was high, blazing down. It was a dry heat, very different from the humid summers Matt knew in Maryland. This wasn't the ideal time to be looking for wildlife. The animals would be resting, waiting out the intense heat of the day. He didn't expect to see any rhinos but was hoping to see some scat or recent tracks. Everything was hot here, Matt thought. Hot and dry. Driving the old Land Rover slowly across the sun-bleached landscape, he turned and headed towards the descending vultures.

Patrick was sitting in the passenger seat beside him. He was the guide Tuhadeli had provided. He was sullen and had been of little help so far. On two occasions, they had crossed the tracks of the desert elephants that called the region home. Patrick had shown little interest or even recognition of what they were. When Matt had got out to look at the spoor, Patrick had remained in the car. Matt doubted he was a tracker at all; more likely, he was just along to keep an eye on him.

"Poachers," Patrick said and nodded toward the vultures. It was as much as he'd said in the last two days. It was what Matt was thinking as well. With the number of vultures, it must be one of the desert elephants or a rhino that had died. Perhaps a giraffe, he hoped. Whether it was a victim of poaching or had died a natural death only the carcass would tell.

Damaraland was a remote region of northwest Namibia, a region that required four-wheel drive. But it was an area where tourists, those who wanted more than a visit to Etosha National Park, would come. If poachers were bold enough to strike here, it was worrying.

Matt ground the clutch as he tried to get into second gear. *Damn*, he thought. A well-maintained vehicle would be on the top of his must-have list for Reddman.

The Land Rover climbed a gentle incline and came around the base of a small hill. The vultures were landing about a quarter of a mile away at the edge of some dense mopane bushland that ran up to a range of rocky hills. Matt turned off the engine and looked at the scene through binoculars. There seemed to be at least a hundred raptors there, and more were arriving. White-backed vultures made up the majority, but there were a few lappet-faced vultures with their red heads and brown wings. There was even an endangered Cape griffon with what looked like a colored leg band. Matt didn't know who was studying Capes in this part of Africa, but, whoever it was, they'd like to know when and where this bird had been sighted. Once he had a photo, he'd pass it along to the avian people at the National Zoo. They would know who to send it to.

There were also a few jackals darting in and out of the throng of birds, tearing at the carcass, grabbing mouthfuls of rotting meat and running off to eat.

From where Matt was, he couldn't identify the carcass, though, from its size, he knew it was either a rhino or a smaller elephant. He reached into the back seat to grab his camera. Opening the door, he looked at Patrick.

"Stay here while I see what we have."

Patrick nodded. "It's poachers. We shouldn't stay here long."

Matt noticed a fleeting look of concern in his eyes. The thought of armed poachers in the area was unsettling, but he needed to document what had happened.

At first glance, Matt wasn't sure what had killed this animal. He needed to see the animal's head to know, and that was hidden by the bulk of the bloated body. He caught the sweet, pungent smell of the rotting animal as a gentle breeze blew by. Patrick was wrong, he thought. They could stay as long as they wanted. The animal had been dead for a while now, at least a day, maybe two. If it was poachers, they would be a long way off. Matt walked away from the Rover. He decided to stay about a hundred yards from the carcass. He wanted to walk a large circle around the carcass since, if it had been killed, he would come across the tracks of whoever had done it: tracks coming and tracks going.

As he walked around, he scanned the ground in front of him, occasionally looking up at the carcass with its throng of scavengers. Then he saw it—one of the animal's feet had three toes. *Damn it, it is a rhino,* he thought, as he swatted a fly from his neck. He lifted his camera and took a couple of pictures, including one of the Cape that had hopped onto the rhino's head and was pecking at an empty eye socket.

He only had to walk a short distance before he could make out the top of the rhino's head. Patrick was right. It was poachers. Both horns had been hacked off the head. The carcass still looked massive, but the hide had been stripped away in a few places, and Matt could see that it had largely been hollowed out already. He lifted his camera again and snapped some more photographs.

It didn't take him long to find tracks leading to and from the dead rhino. He walked back to the Land Rover.

"I've found some tracks, and I'm going to follow them. Are you coming with me?"

Patrick looked ill. He took a handkerchief out of his pocket and wiped his brow. "No, Matt. I will stay here and watch the truck."

Chapter 4

On his way back to the human tracks, Matt walked by the rhino carcass again, this time coming closer to snap some more photos with his digital camera. The rhino had died at the edge of the bush. It was a disturbing sight. A few vultures eyed him warily, but he hadn't yet moved so close that they'd give up their prize. The jackals, milling around the fringes of the carcass, paid little attention.

The carcass was a broken, bloated remnant of the animal that had, just a couple of days earlier, been browsing its way through the landscape. The smell of death hung over the area, amplified by the intense heat. He pondered who might have done this. The local police? That wouldn't surprise him. They were probably underpaid, poorly trained and easily corrupted. The people who actually carried out the poaching received only a fraction of the final price of the horn, he knew, but even that would seem like a vast sum in an impoverished area like this. If it were the police, they would have a ready-made network to transport the horn out of the country.

Matt looked down at the tracks left by the poachers. Simple footprints, but he knew that following them could take him in any number of directions. Whoever he found at the end of the tracks was not likely to appreciate his curiosity. But the poaching needed to stop. Two rhinos from the Damaraland population dead in the space of a few weeks was unsustainable. Collecting genetic material was going to be difficult enough, and if organized poaching existed in the area, it might be impossible. The poaching would have to be dealt with first. He knew tracking poachers wasn't why he was here. He could turn back and report what he had found, but to whom, and what would be done if he did report it? If Tuhadeli and Reddman were correct and the police were involved, Matt did not want to advertise his presence.

Matt knelt down next to the tracks and sketched out a small box in the sand roughly the size of his own stride. He then counted the footprints inside the box. Three poachers, he estimated, traveling at a walk. Some loose sand had blown over the prints. *These are still visible, but they certainly aren't fresh*, he thought. That just confirmed what the rhino carcass had already told him: the poachers had been gone a while. He slung his camera over his shoulder and began to walk into the mopane bushland, his hunting rifle in hand.

* * *

Patrick sat in the passenger seat of the Land Rover watching Matt recede. Sweat trickled down the back of his neck and soaked his T-shirt. A lone fly landed and wandered across his cheek. He didn't notice.

He wanted to be away from this place, away from the dead rhino, away from the poachers. He took a deep breath. He knew why they were here. Tuhadeli wanted the American to discover the poachers and either get rid of them or die. Patrick didn't want to die. He didn't want to see the American die. He had seen enough of death fighting for SWAPO's armed wing in southern Angola. The People's Liberation Army of Namibia, like many liberation movements, had been a poor fighting force, but, as a guerrilla organization, it had managed some successes. Patrick had endured ten years of training and fighting in the bush, ten years of moving camp, trying to stay one step ahead of the South African patrols. Every rainy season, when PLAN had infiltrated South West Africa from its bases in Angola, the South Africans had been waiting. They had been relentless, appearing out of nowhere, killing without remorse. After the intense firefights, the PLAN fighters had usually turned and run away, melting into the bush, avoiding direct contact. They were Cuban trained but in battle had been no match for the professional South African Army. They had had some advantages: the land and the people were theirs, and vanishing was second nature.

Patrick remembered the friends he had lost during those years. They were all Kolonkadhi, members of the Owambo people of northern Namibia and southern Angola. There had been a time when he and his family had lived in relative peace near Oshakati, but that seemed like a lifetime ago. He tried to remember those days before he had been recruited into SWAPO, but he had trouble even picturing his brothers. It had been many years since he had seen them. The war had changed him, and he couldn't bring himself to go home. He was ashamed of what he had done.

He could still see the faces of his comrades who had died, though they mostly came to him in his dreams, reaching out to ask him why he had survived while they had perished. He could not remember when he had last slept a full night. But theirs were not the faces that woke him.

He had hated the whites for what they had done, and for what they had made him do. Late one summer, on patrol fifteen miles south of the Angolan town of Xangongo, his unit had been attacked by a motorized patrol of South Africans. The engines of the Buffel armored personnel carriers as they had lurched through the bush to drop off soldiers had provided the first warning. The battle had been confusing, with men running and firing at anything that moved. Patrick, his AK-47 at his hip, had heard something move behind him. He had turned and sprayed the bush without looking. Time had passed in slow motion after that, the sounds of the battle muffled and distant. He had searched the area once he had stopped shooting and had found a South African soldier lying in a pool of blood. Patrick's AK-47 had almost cut him in half, just above the waist. The soldier had dropped his gun and was lying there with a look of disbelief on his face as he tried to stop the wounds from bleeding. Patrick had knelt down next to him as the soldier had reached out one blood-soaked hand for Patrick to grasp. Patrick had taken it and looked into his face. It was the face of a boy, the face of a teenager. It was only for a moment, and then the blue eyes had glazed over. It was those blue eyes that he woke to every morning. There had been no hate in them, just confusion, fear and then nothing.

His comrades had found him there and dragged him away from the body and the battle as the South Africans had pushed forward. They had run hard and long, wanting to put as much distance between themselves and the soldiers as possible. When they had stopped for the night, they had still been able to hear the occasional sounds of distant gunfire. They had not lit a fire, and each man had found a place in the dense bush to sleep in as well as he could. Patrick, awake, had crouched under a large acacia tree with his knees to his chest against the cold night air and had watched the sky. A thousand stars were shining brightly. They were the same stars that his father had looked upon, and his father before him. They had always looked down on the Owambo, cold and unchanging. As Patrick had stared, the war had grown small, insignificant. Where once he had had belief, only questions had remained.

Why had such a young man been sent to this place to die? And why had Patrick been there to do the killing? He had been as willing as anyone to kill the South Africans. It had been easy. To fire from a distance, detached. Killing the boy had changed that. The blood pumping out of ragged bullet holes, the struggle for breath and the bright, blue eyes: it had been personal, intimate, senseless. Later, when his comrades were sleeping, exhausted from the battle and long retreat, Patrick had leaned his AK-47 against the trunk of the tree and walked south, away from Angola, away from the war, away from the boy. He had stopped hating that night.

In the years that had followed, Patrick had traveled through much of Namibia, looking for work, never staying long in one place. He had worked briefly on a small fishing trawler out of Walvis Bay and had spent several years as a farm laborer on different cattle farms. Before coming to Khorixas, he had spent a short time working in an abattoir. His co-workers had developed a deep indifference to the work, but Patrick had found the killing factory disturbing. With his brothers, he had protected his family's herd as a child, driving the cattle from one place to another, looking for grazing and water and returning the cattle to the family's compound before the sun set. The abattoir had been a slaughter machine where the cattle had been processed efficiently, without feeling or compassion, for markets in Europe. His co-workers had laughed and joked as they had gone about their daily work, but Patrick had kept to himself, quietly appalled at the work he was doing. This was where a former PLAN comrade had introduced him to Tuhadeli, who had been hiring former PLAN members to return with him to Khorixas. As poorly paid as it was, Patrick was grateful for the work and for the opportunity to get away from the slaughterhouse. The money allowed him to rent a small room from an old lady who lived on the edge of the town. It wasn't much, and if he wanted to wash, he had to walk to a communal tap and wait in line. There was a small cot in the room, but he rarely slept on it, preferring the hard-packed dirt floor. For a pillow, he used an old coat. Before the war, he had slept in a bed, but after, he preferred the feel of the earth; a roof over his head was comfort enough.

The American is brave, Patrick thought. *Brave or foolish*.

The American was right about the rhino having been dead for at least a day or two, and the poachers were probably gone from the area, but that didn't mean they were safe. The passing of time hadn't saved the other man who had been out here looking for the poachers. The one whose body had been dumped overnight in Khorixas had been an ex-PLAN fighter. He had been a man who had known the area and the animals. But he was now dead. And he had suffered before he had died. Patrick had seen the body.

It was rumored around town that an old enemy had

returned and was now behind the poaching. There was no proof, but it was said that members of 32 Battalion, the Buffalos, had returned to Namibia. 32 Battalion had had a fearsome reputation in southern Angola during the fight for independence. Made up of South Africans, former Rhodesians, English veterans and South West Africans, the Buffalos had been mercenaries, born to fight. If the rumors were true, it was not good news. Patrick did not want to revisit the war in any way. He had tried to forget it, but it had followed him everywhere, the killing a deep stain he could not wash away.

Patrick brushed at the fly that was now on his lips. Matt had told him he would track for an hour and then return to the truck. The American had taken a hunting rifle out of the back of the Land Rover. That had surprised Patrick and left him uneasy. It had been many years since he had held a gun, and he found even the sight of one discomforting. Matt had taken some water, but he did not have the supplies to track the poachers for long; he had said he only wanted to get an idea of the direction they might have headed. Patrick looked at the carcass of the rhino, now being swarmed over by the vultures. It would be gone before long. There had been too much death in Patrick's life already. The war had removed his hate, but had left nothing in its place. He had tried to hide from the emptiness, but sitting here, looking at another dead animal, an animal that had not needed to die, Patrick felt a twinge of anger.

He couldn't do anything about the friends he had lost in the war. He couldn't do anything about the young South African soldier he had gunned down. He couldn't even do anything about the rhino that now lay dead in front of him. But he could help the American. He was tired of walking away. He opened the door to the Land Rover and started after Matt at a jog.

* * *

Half an hour passed, and the tracks were still easy to follow. Whoever had killed the rhino wasn't too worried about being followed.

Matt stopped a moment to survey the land ahead. The tracks ran in a straight line, out of the stand of thick mopane trees through which he had been walking into the dried bed of a seasonal river. The bed of the river fanned out, wide, shallow and sandy. It ran by the base of two hills to his left. The first hill partly shielded his view of the second, larger hill, but both looked rocky and barren from where he stood. He would need to turn back soon, but he wanted to follow the tracks beyond the two hills. It was unlikely the poachers had traveled too far on foot, and he suspected he'd find vehicle tracks before too long.

He was about to walk on when he heard a whistle to his back. He looked around quickly. About fifty yards behind him, Patrick was kneeling and with a downward motion of his hand was indicating that Matt should do the same. When Matt had dropped down, Patrick waved for him to come back. Matt jogged back in a crouch.

"What's going on?" Matt asked as he knelt down next to Patrick, surprised that he had shown up.

"This is not good," Patrick said. "The tracks are too easy."

"That's true," Matt smiled. "But they are old, at least a day or two."

"You can read spoor." Patrick smiled back. It was the

first time Matt could remember seeing him smile. "That is good, but do you know who you are hunting?"

"Poachers. Who else would I be tracking?"

"How many poachers?"

"Three. There are three sets of tracks."

"I think two," Patrick said, "with a third man tracking them ahead of us."

"Are you sure?"

"Come walk with me. We will come at this in a new way and see if we can learn something we do not yet know."

Matt looked back at the hills, the larger, more distant one almost completely hidden behind the smaller one. The larger hill had a clear view of the whole riverbed. They turned back, walked for ten minutes parallel to the base of the smaller hill and then turned directly towards the slope. When they reached the foot of the hill, Patrick stopped and knelt down again.

Matt sat on a rock with his rifle across his thigh. "You know who is poaching the rhinos, don't you?" Matt asked.

Patrick looked at him for a moment before answering. "No. But it is being said that it is soldiers."

"Soldiers? The Namibian Army is doing this?" Matt asked, astounded.

"No. The Buffalos, 32 Battalion from South Africa, have returned and are doing the killing. They are old soldiers who fought against us in the years of the war."

"How do you know? And why wouldn't Jonathan have told me?"

"I do not know. It is only being said. Tuhadeli has many reasons for doing many things. Be careful with him."

Matt sat back and thought for a moment. He took his

canteen out and took a quick mouthful of the water. He offered the canteen to Patrick, who took a swallow.

"So, why did you stop me from tracking the poachers?"

"I think, if you had walked into the riverbed, you would have been shot."

Matt stared at him in disbelief. "Shot?"

"Yes," Patrick said. "I have seen this before. Many times we tracked the South Africans, and many more times they tracked us. If the tracks are easy to follow, it is not a good thing. I think if we climb this hill, we shall learn if you were about to die."

The slope was steep and strewn with rocks. Before he started to climb after Patrick, Matt doubled-checked his gun to make sure it wasn't loaded. The last thing he wanted was an accidental discharge. It was a habit whenever he was in challenging terrain. As they neared the top, Patrick lay down and started to crawl, making sure he kept a low profile as he crested the hill. Matt came up next to him. As they lay there, they had a clear view of the larger hill beyond and the wide, sandy riverbed that ran along the base of both hills.

Matt scanned the nearby hill but didn't see anything. Like the hill they were on, it was unremarkable and covered in rocks and gravel. He was about to say something when Patrick reached out and touched his arm. He then pointed to an area just below the crest of the other hill. Matt looked again, at first not seeing anything, and then discerning a small movement. There was a man sitting with his back towards a large rock, partially hidden in shadow. Matt reached around his back for his camera, slowly bringing it up to his face. Using the zoom lens, he focused in on the stranger.

He was a white man in brown clothing, clothing that blended well with the parched hillside. He wore a wide-brimmed hat to keep himself shaded from the sun, and across his lap rested a rifle with a hunting scope. Matt snapped a photo and then focused as well as he could on the man's face. It was weathered brown and unshaven. His shirt was soaked in sweat, despite the shade he was sitting in. Matt saw him take a drink of water, but other than that, he sat still. The brim of his hat covered his eyes as he looked down over the riverbed, patiently watching, patiently waiting. Matt snapped another photo. *This is another hunter,* he thought, *sitting still with his own thoughts, waiting for his prey to come to him.* Matt had spent many hours in the woods of Maryland doing just what this man was doing, the only difference being the prey.

Patrick touched his arm and indicated they should move away, back down the side of the hill, where they would be hidden. Moving slowly, they both dropped below the crest until they were completely hidden from sight. They moved carefully down the hill, being sure not to kick up any dust.

"I think you would be dead now," Patrick said.

Matt looked at him. "I think you might be right." He paused. "How did you know about this? Who was the other tracker?"

Patrick looked hard at Matt. "He was a man Tuhadeli had sent out to search for poachers. His body was dumped in Khorixas overnight. I saw it there this morning."

Matt sat down again to think. He hadn't expected to find a poacher while he tracked, perhaps the poachers' tracks and the route they had taken into the area, but not an actual person. The man apparently had no qualms about killing. He also possessed some discipline. To sit for a day or two waiting in ambush for somebody who might or might not come took patience, and it spoke of a deeper motive than just killing a rhino. With one death already and a death trap set, the poachers were sending a message.

"Thanks for stopping me," Matt said and breathed in deeply.

Patrick nodded.

The man had been here for a while, Matt judged, probably since the poaching incident. He looked back. In the distance, he could see a couple of vultures still landing and a few, now sated, leaving. He knew they would fly miles before they roosted for the night. The man was probably going to stay until the vultures stopped coming in to feast. The raptors were what had drawn Matt and Patrick to the rhino carcass. Once the scavengers were gone, it would be pure chance that someone would happen across the remains.

There were a few hours left in the day, so it was unlikely the man would move. Matt took out his canteen again. It was getting close to being empty. Water was the key to surviving in this barren place. The man had been sweating, and he had taken a drink. If he was planning on staying until the vultures stopped flying in, then he must have some sort of base nearby, somewhere where he kept his water.

"I think we should find where this man sleeps and where he keeps his water," Matt said to Patrick.

It didn't take them too long to find it. They tracked around the back of the hills, and there, a quarter of a mile away near a small strand of euphorbia bushes, was the man's truck. They approached it along the line of bushes, doing their best in the barren landscape to stay under cover. As they got near, they saw that the man had been careful not to set up much of a camp. When he left, he needed to be able to do so quickly and leave little evidence that he had been there. Matt guessed he slept in the truck.

"We need to make him leave the area, so he doesn't harm anyone else who might happen by," Matt said as they knelt next to one of the bushes.

"Give me your water and stay here," Patrick said and then quickly moved towards the truck. Matt surveyed the crest of the hill. There was no movement, just the sun beating down on hard ground and brown rocks.

Matt glanced back at Patrick, who had already hopped into the bed of the truck and was kneeling down. Matt couldn't see what he was doing. He looked up at the hill. Still nothing. Matt took out his camera and took some pictures of the truck. It was a nondescript white Toyota that was covered in dust, a familiar sight on Namibia's roads. Matt had already seen several like it in his short time in the country. He zoomed in on the license plate and snapped two more photos.

Patrick was now back on the ground, but moving slowly back to the euphorbia bushes as he carefully dusted over his own tracks, leaving no evidence of his presence.

"We should go now," he said when he had rejoined Matt.

On the trek back, they went slowly at first, continuing to mask their own tracks until they reached the point where they had climbed the hill. If this man was ex-South African military, they didn't want him to know that he had been discovered.

"What did you do in the truck?" Matt asked when they had made it back to the Land Rover.

Patrick handed the now full canteen back to Matt. "I filled this with water," he smiled, a broad grin spreading across his face. "And I loosened the cap on his can of water.

It is leaking into the back of his truck, where the sun will burn it off. It will all be gone in an hour. Our friend will have a very thirsty drive home, I think."

Chapter 5

Silke DuPlessis sat in the *Namibian Star*'s newsroom, thinking about the dramatic turn her life had taken in the last two weeks. She took a sip of her coffee; she liked it black and sweet. It was early in the morning, and the newsroom was empty and quiet. She preferred getting to the office before the sun came up. It was a vestige of her childhood in South Africa's Eastern Cape where she had been up early each day to help her parents open their general store in the small town of Craddock. Her parents had worked hard and had managed to help her get her degree in journalism at Rhodes University in Grahamstown. It was there she had met Karl Ritchie at a small conference being hosted by the university. Karl was the publisher of the *Namibian Star* and had recruited her to come north to write for the paper.

That was seven years ago and Silke was starting to feel that she'd outgrown the paper. She had built a solid portfolio and was now looking to use it to step back to South Africa. She had outgrown Karl as well. He had taken her as a lover when she had first arrived in Windhoek, seeing her on days they both worked late and then returning to his wife and three children in the exclusive suburbs of Klein Windhoek. She had given in quite willingly. It had been an exciting time: new job, new city, new lover. As the years had passed, the late night work sessions had grown fewer. Now when they were together, it was comfortable and predictable, and each sensed the relationship had run its course. Early on, she had envisioned him leaving his wife, but now she knew he was too settled to take that step.

She took another sip of coffee and smiled at the memory. The thought seemed silly now. Karl was never going leave his wife, the *Namibian Star* or Windhoek. It had been a childish fantasy, one in which she realized she had no lasting interest. She would look back on these years with Karl with a great deal of fondness. He had taught her much about being a woman and being a journalist, but it was time to move on with her life.

That brought her back to thinking about the dramatic change that had occurred. As good as her portfolio was, she needed a high-profile story, a story that would separate her from the other candidates at small provincial papers across southern Africa who were looking to move on in their careers. As a reporter, her beat included the environment and wildlife. Her contacts at the Ministry of Wildlife had kept her informed about the export of the black rhino to America, but that story had been given little more than a footnote in the paper. Her editor hadn't seen any news in it. The routine transport of an animal, even when endangered, rarely made headlines. The slaughter of the rhino in America had been global news, and she had been given considerable space to report on the local reaction. But even that story had been local in focus and, outside of Namibia, had merited little interest. That's when the package from America had arrived. The package that had changed everything.

* * *

She had emptied the contents onto her desk. It had taken her a moment to process what she was seeing. The photos that had tumbled out were crime scene photos from the Baltimore City Zoo in Maryland. They had shown the dead rhino lying in a pool of blood, its horns missing, cut off at the base. They had also shown the headless corpse of the woman who had died, lying front down, tranquilizer gun on the ground next to her. There were other images: a photo of a burnt-out car in an empty lot, a photo of another headless corpse and several photos of two guns, a pistol and some sort of shotgun.

She had looked back inside the envelope. There had been a document that had explained the photos, but nothing to identify who had sent the package. The note was sterile and to the point, the photos graphic. Silke had been sure right away that Karl would have a field day laying out the front page. The most shocking items had been the identification of the guns as South African military models and the identification of the second body as the probable killer of the rhino and the woman. Silke had quickly put all the material back into the envelope and had then gone online. She had been following the international news closely since the story had broken and until now had seen nothing tying the crime to South Africa. Online, she had done a quick survey of all the major American web pages, going to the newspaper sites first: *The New York Times*, *The Washington Post*, the *Chicago Tribune* and, finally, *The Sun* in Baltimore. Nothing new on the rhino death. She had then checked the major American networks, CNN, CBS, ABC, NBC and FOX. Still nothing new. Finally, she had gone to the major

49

South African news sites, the *Herald* and SABCTV. They had had no coverage either.

She had sat back in her chair with a growing sense of excitement. She had known then that she had the exclusive she had been looking for: crime scene photos from Baltimore that had not been released broadly to the press, an identification of the guns as being South African military models and an indication that the person who had shot the rhino had been killed and decapitated. This was an explosive story that could tie the violent crime in America back to South Africa and Namibia. The story could go in any number of directions: Who had killed the rhino in America, and why had the killer used South African military guns? Was there a South African military connection with rhino poaching on the continent? If so, did this tie into a larger story of political corruption in Namibia and South Africa? The questions had raced through her mind as she had started to frame the story she would write.

Karl had initially been cautious. They hadn't known who had sent the pictures, and unconfirmed sources always worried him, especially on big stories. But what had worried him more had been their inability to get any sort of useful response from the Baltimore City Police Department. They had called on a number of occasions and had been told that the department had no comment about ongoing investigations and had not released any images to the media. Despite that, Karl had believed the package was genuine. He said he had seen many photos of death over his career, and he could tell right away these were real. That had not stopped him from worrying about why the *Namibian Star* had received the photos while larger media organizations apparently had not. His whole career had been in newspapers, and he had a keen sense of when he was being played. Still, Silke had been insistent that they run the story quickly, before any other outlets. Despite his worries, he had agreed. She was not surprised. Stories like this drove circulation, and that in turn would lead to more advertising dollars.

A couple of days after the story had run, the phone had started to ring. Media organizations around the world had wanted access to the photos and to Silke's story. It had been a heady few days. The story had revitalized interest in the rhino story just when it had almost faded out of the news cycle. Everyone had wanted to know who was behind the killing of the two Americans and the Baltimore City Zoo's rhino, and they were looking to Silke to discover the answer.

* * *

Karl was next to arrive at the office. He found Silke in the staff kitchen making her second cup of coffee.

"Make me one and drop by my office. We need to talk," he said.

Silke smiled. "I'll be there in a minute."

Karl's office was small and sparsely decorated. He had had a long career at the paper, a career that had spanned the three decades since the paper had been founded. In those early years, the war of independence years, the staff at the *Namibian Star* had worked tirelessly to expose the human rights violations of the South African Defense Forces. The paper's unpopular editorial stance had led to boycotts by the white community, and its offices had even been attacked by a right-wing Afrikaner group. But the paper and its reporters had endured. After independence, the paper had turned its critical focus on the new SWAPO government, which in turn had led to a short-lived boycott by the new government. It was a time that Silke knew Karl looked back on with a great deal of pride. The paper was small, and would never rival some of the larger dailies in the region, but it had a proud tradition of seeking and printing the truth, of serving the people of Namibia whoever was in power.

"We've opened up a can of worms with this story, you know," Karl said as Silke walked into his office and handed him his cup.

"Yes, we have," Silke replied. She had been expecting to have this conversation with Karl for a day or two. She knew he had published early because of her, and she knew the story needed further work: a follow-up feature that would explain the why, the how and the who behind the rhino killing in Baltimore. Her feature had added a layer of detail to what had already been reported, but the rest was still a mystery.

"I don't regret publishing it. We don't get a worldwide exclusive every day," he continued. "But not knowing the source for that material still bothers me. We should have taken more time to make sure the editorial foundation of the story was stronger, that it would stand up to intense scrutiny. We need to correct that now."

"How do you think we should approach it?" she asked.

"I've been thinking about that. On the face of it, the key new bit of information is the South African military connection. Why were the guns used South African military models? I'm sure you can buy whatever guns you want in America if you're willing to pay the price, but it seems to me that getting two South African guns to kill an endangered animal from southern Africa in America is more than a coincidence. The young man who is the main suspect in the killing is black. How did he get the guns? Who are the people who set him up to commit the crime? And why was he killed afterwards? That's the angle I'd take if I was one of the major news organizations in America or South Africa. They would have the resources and contacts, both in America and here, to start investigating that line of inquiry."

"But we have a problem with that, don't we?" The *Namibian Star* had a proud history of critical reporting on those in power, but it was a small paper with a small budget. Silke and Karl both knew that there was no money to send her to South Africa, let alone America, to try to track down the guns and how they had made it into the killer's hands.

"Yes, we do," Karl answered. "We either got lucky with that package or we are being manipulated, and I don't really believe in luck."

"Why would someone want to manipulate us? They could get a much larger impact with the story by leaking this material to any number of other news organizations."

Karl looked at her for a moment. Silke recognized what Karl was up to. She had answered her own question. It was a game they had played any number of times over the last few years.

"Okay, whoever it was didn't want to make a big splash, at least not immediately. Once we had published, the news would spread, but it would take a day or two for other news organizations to pick up on what we published," she reasoned.

"Seems about right to me," Karl said. "So, why send us the images then?"

Silke put her lips to the rim of her cup and blew softly. "The only reason to send the material to us would be to reach a small audience, a Namibian audience. But who and why? And how do we find out?"

"I don't know the who or the why, but I have an idea about the how. We don't have the resources or the contacts to trace the guns, but we do have the key to this whole thing: the black rhinos."

"The rhinos? That seems a pretty straightforward poaching story to me, one that we, along with everyone else, have already written," Silke interjected.

"Everyone has written about the poaching angle, true, but I think we are missing something there. Why else would we have received that package? We've written the boilerplate story about why these and other rhinos are being poached, the same story that has been in newspapers all over the world, but I think there are deeper, hidden currents here. There's a story that we aren't seeing because we haven't looked closely enough. If you want a job at the *Herald* in Johannesburg, that's the story that will get it for you."

Silke looked at Karl. She wasn't really surprised that he had guessed she was looking to leave. She knew him well enough to know he was extremely perceptive. "How long have you known that I want to leave?"

"I've known all along that you would. It was just a matter of time. The *Namibian Star* has been my life's work, and Windhoek my home, but for you, it was always going to be a stepping-stone to larger things. This story will get you back to South Africa, but you need to wrap it up in the right way. You had the big easy splash with the photos, but now you need to do the hard investigative work to find out what is really going on with these rhinos. You need to go to Damaraland."

Chapter 6

Steven Reddman walked down the hallway of his San Diego home and stepped out onto the balcony. He had just received an e-mail from Tuhadeli telling him about the article in the *Namibian Star* and saying that Matthew Harkes had seen it. If Harkes knew about a South African military connection to the rhino, Reddman wondered what he would do about it.

Reddman was not surprised that a small-town newspaper like the *Namibian Star* had leapt at the chance to run the photos. *Provincial hacks*, he thought. Reconsidering, he realized that was unkind, since most of the major news media organizations would have done the same in a rush for circulation, ratings and advertising dollars. He held them all in contempt. Getting the photos from the Baltimore City Police Department had been the biggest challenge, but money was a powerful incentive. It was then a simple matter of finding the weak link, in this case a lieutenant coming up to retirement who had been passed over for promotion.

Reddman looked out across the Pacific Ocean towards Asia. *That is the future*, he thought. Countries like China, Vietnam and Thailand with growing middle classes, growing wealth. Those were the countries that offered real opportunities. America, like Europe, was stagnant, a spent force weighed down by debt.

He took in a deep breath of the cool ocean air and thought back to his time in Vietnam. That had been a special time in his life. He had served with the military police in Saigon during the Vietnam War. He had loved the city with its wide boulevards, French colonial era buildings and chaotic traffic. If the war hadn't been lost, he might have stayed.

"Darling, why don't you come down and join me? The water is wonderful."

Reddman looked down from the balcony. Cecile, his wife, was slipping into the pool. Tall, blonde and statuesque, she was still beautiful despite her age.

"I'll be down in a few minutes. I've got some work to finish in my office, and I want to check on the arrangements for tonight."

He had met Cecile Bezuidenhout in South Africa while he had been the director of the San Diego Zoological Park. He had been traveling with a group of zoo directors on a four-week safari through three southern African countries. Her family owned and ran a series of game lodges and ranches that catered to the high-end safari and hunting markets. He hadn't married her for love, but over the years he had found himself growing increasingly possessive. She had not seemed to mind. Reddman kept her in the style to which she was accustomed. She had grown up wealthy and had retained a taste for luxury, traveling regularly between the west coast of America and her family's home in Kwa-Zulu Natal. It was a gilded cage, but a cage in which she seemed content.

The San Diego Zoological Park had had southern white rhinos in its collection at the time, but it hadn't been until Reddman had been married for a year that he had begun to take a deeper interest in the species. Cecile's family's ranches had been cattle farms, but with the growing tourist market and uncertain beef prices, they had diversified and had started to restock the land with wild animals that had been hunted out years before. The flagship species was the white rhino. Over the years, the family had purchased a growing number of excess animals from South African Parks Department auctions.

Jannie, Cecile's younger brother, had taken Reddman on a tour of the family's game ranches. Like Reddman, he had served in the military, having spent ten years in the South African Defense Force before returning home to run the family's business. He and Reddman had bonded quickly. Reddman had been struck by the growing population of white rhinos under the family's control. He had spent many late nights discussing the wildlife business with Jannie, and it was by these campfires that his vision for rhinos had started to take form. At first it had been small in scope, but with time it had grown.

Reddman watched Cecile as she slipped under the water and began to swim to the far end of the pool. Her long, platinum-blonde hair and deeply tanned body glimmered as the sunlight danced off the ripples in the water. She had been a real asset in San Diego society, helping him establish a reputation as a leader in global conservation and an astute businessman. They were one of the city's most popular power couples and were in demand at social and fundraising events throughout the year. Later that night, they were hosting a black-tie dinner at their home for local dignitaries and a group of businessmen and bankers from China.

Cecile surfaced at the far end of the pool and ran her hands across her face and along the sides of her head, wiping the water away. She glanced up at him and stuck her tongue out. He smiled and walked back to his office. That day's mail and a courier package were sitting on his desk unopened. He needed to deal with these routine matters, but first he wanted to check on the arrangements for dinner.

He walked downstairs to the kitchen. Maria was with two of the assistants he had hired for the day. She was marinating the beef for the night's dinner.

"How's everything coming along?" he asked.

Maria had been with them for ten years. She did the cooking and ran the house. She was a second generation Mexican-American who was almost family.

"Very well, señor Steven," she replied. "Who are we having over tonight?"

"The usual crowd and some very important colleagues from China," he replied with a serious tone. "So don't overcook anything like you usually do."

Maria laughed. "Overcook dinner? You are mistaking me for your wife."

She was right. Cecile was a hopeless cook.

"Just keep Cecile away from the rice if she comes in to help or it will end up lumpy and we may well have an international incident. You know what she's like."

He left the kitchen and checked the dining room table. It had been set earlier in the day, but he wanted to make sure that everything was in place, that everything would be perfect for his guests that evening.

Reddman returned to his office and sat down in his

chair. Putting the mail to one side, he opened the courier package. He pushed the packing material out of the way, then took a deep, slow breath and closed his eyes. Opening them, he stared again at the contents. Inside the box were two skulls. Towards the back of one of them was a round hole. He felt goose bumps rise on the back of his neck, and he shuddered.

When the house had been built in San Diego, Reddman had had a special "safe" room built that could only be accessed through his office. The heavy security door had an electronic lock that was opened with a password that only he knew. Reddman quickly reclosed the package, picked it up and walked over to the security door. He keyed in the password, walked into the room and put the package on a shelf. Closing the door behind him, he walked back down the hallway to the balcony.

Cecile was now lying, face down, on a beach towel laid out on the grass. She sensed he was looking and glanced up.

"Are you coming down?"

"Why don't you come up and meet me in the bedroom?" he countered.

She saw the gleam in his eye and grinned. "I'll be right up, you beast."

Chapter 7

Tuhadeli looked through Matt's photographs again. They showed a dead rhino, a small white pickup truck in the desert and a man sitting on a hill with a rifle.

"Together, these are damning," Tuhadeli said. "They will certainly be enough to get the police's attention, but I am still hesitant to take the images to them. There is a good possibility that the local police might be involved in the poaching, and if so, I don't want them to know about these."

Matt nodded. "What can we do then?" he asked. "Would taking them to the police in larger centers be better?"

"Probably," Tuhadeli agreed. "But it wouldn't hurt to try to find out even more before you do that. I was able to track down the license plate on the white truck. The truck is registered to a Pik Malan in Ruacana, a small town on Namibia's northwest border with Angola."

*   *   *

Matt was in the Land Rover with Patrick, driving west, away from Khorixas. As they put the town behind them, the land became more arid and empty. The scope of what Reddman wanted was growing increasingly apparent.

The land was vast and barren. Finding any rhino might take days of tracking. Trying to collect genetic material from the whole population was going to be extremely difficult and expensive. It had been easy to think of the difficulties that a project like this would run into while sitting at his desk in the rhino building at the National Zoo in Washington, DC. It had also been easy to imagine solutions. Now that he was driving through Damaraland, the difficulties loomed larger, and the solutions seemed increasingly inadequate.

Even this preliminary stage of the project would have been easier if I had been in touch with the local Namibian wildlife experts, Matt thought. *Or at least a non-profit wildlife group with people who know the area and the animals.*

But Tuhadeli had again voiced concerns and reminded Matt that Reddman wanted to keep this off the Ministry of Wildlife Conservation's radar until they were sure that collecting genetic material would be feasible. Reaching out to any one of these groups, especially if it was done by a zoo-based group from the United States, would lead to a slew of questions being asked, and perhaps the shutting down of Matt's trip into Damaraland. Given the strained relations after the Maryland incident, it was perhaps best to carry out the low-key preliminary assessment in obscurity.

With an active poaching ring in the area, Matt was uncomfortable not knowing who could be trusted, and he didn't want to tip his hand to anyone who might be involved. He had left his meeting with Tuhadeli frustrated. The man had struck him as a politician with little experience with wildlife issues.

"What did Tuhadeli tell you?" Patrick asked.

Matt looked at his new friend. *So much for first*

impressions, he thought. In the few days since they had found the rhino carcass and Patrick had saved his life, the man had hardly stopped speaking. Not that Matt minded. It was a relief to have someone to talk to in this open and quiet country. There was a radio in the Land Rover, but it was broken. Patrick assured him that, even if it was new, they would not be able to get any stations where they were going anyway.

"Well, I think he was a bit surprised to see me walk through the door," Matt said, drumming his fingers on the steering wheel. "He was interested in the dead rhino, and also in the photos we took of the man and the truck. He didn't want to go to the police, and he's probably right there. He thinks they might be involved in the poaching. You know that I am here to do an initial assessment of the area and the rhino population, but I think it is going to fall to me, fall to us, if you are up to helping me, to find out what is happening to these rhinos."

Patrick looked out the window, peering off into the distance. There was no reason Patrick should want to help him, Matt realized. He had no overriding reason to be interested in the wellbeing of the Damaraland rhinos. He was just in the Land Rover because it was a job in a land with few jobs. It was obvious he wasn't being paid well. He wore the same shorts and worn-out T-shirt every day. Matt guessed he was mildly malnourished and probably ate only once a day. Tuhadeli had asked him to accompany Matt on his assessment of the area, but that assignment hadn't included a possible run-in with dangerous poachers. It was a lot for Matt to ask, but he hoped Patrick would agree to help. A few moments of silence passed as Matt left Patrick with his own thoughts.

When Patrick spoke, he did so without looking back into the truck. "These are bad people who should be stopped. We will try to stop them together. But I must tell you, I will not kill anyone."

It was the answer Matt had been hoping for, but he was surprised that Patrick had brought up the possibility of having to kill someone. Despite the encounter with the poacher on the hillside, the thought of actually killing someone had not crossed his mind. He wanted to discover what was going on with the rhinos and to help bring it to an end without hurting anyone. They drove on in silence for several miles before Matt spoke again.

"I came here to save life, not to take it."

Patrick looked at him and nodded.

That night, they parked the Land Rover at the base of a hill and made camp. The going had been slow after they had left the road. The terrain was rugged and made for difficult driving. Even with a four-wheel-drive vehicle, it had been exhausting. Matt had yet to decide how best to track rhinos in the desert. The animals ranged across huge expanses of land looking for water and forage. They had been driving all day and had seen no evidence of rhino.

They set up camp, Matt breaking out a small tent he had brought along for the trip and erecting it on the west-facing side of the vehicle. He wanted it to be in the shade when the sun came up in the morning. Patrick cleared out a space in the back of the Land Rover. When the camp was settled, Matt got out the stove and cooked a dinner of canned beef and beans. He was no great chef, but they were both hungry and gulped the meal down.

* * *

Patrick tried to get to sleep, but found himself unsettled. Being unable to sleep was not new, but this time it was different. For years, his nights had been tortured by dreams of the war, haunted by the faces of his friends who hadn't survived and always ending with the clear, blue eyes of the young South African soldier he had gunned down. The dreams had persisted, adding to the deep sense of emptiness that had pervaded his life. He had been searching for years for something to fill the void left by the war.

Patrick got out of the Land Rover and climbed onto the roof rack so he could lie down with a clear view of the African sky. As he lay there, staring up at a thousand stars, he realized things were different, and he was struggling to understand why. He looked down at the tent where Matt was sleeping. Things had changed the day they had tracked the poacher.

When he traveled, or when he started a new job, he would try to fit in, try to be normal. But he knew that he was different. His friends would have wives or girlfriends to go home to, but he could not relate. He would go to local shabeens for a drink, but he always felt detached from the crowd. He would have a drink or two before leaving alone. During the SWAPO training, he had learned to hate the white South Africans, and he had fought and killed, that hate a driving force. The blue-eyed boy had changed that, stripping away his anger and showing him the futility of all the killing, but the incident had not replaced the anger with anything.

That had all changed the moment he had stepped out of the Land Rover and followed Matt tracking the poachers. That had been the moment he had started to feel alive again.

Why was this American here, and why did he care about

the rhinos? Patrick had seen rhinos on occasion when he was young, but only from a distance, and he hadn't thought twice about them. They were part of the landscape, much like the zebra, gemsbok and kudu. They were large and fast, and when he did see them, he knew to stay away. Beyond that, they were nothing to him.

He hadn't thought about rhinos since, until Tuhadeli had told him he would be going into the desert with an American. At the time, Patrick had hesitated. Everyone in Khorixas knew that Tuhadeli had already sent another man out into the desert to investigate what was happening to the rhinos. Now he was being asked to do the same thing. He had known he would have to go, as Tuhadeli was the only person in town he could get work from. If he had refused, he would not have been paid again, and he would have had to move on. But he had nowhere else to go. The only option left was home, but he knew he wasn't ready to do that. How would his family receive him? They were deeply religious, steeped in the Lutheran Church. They had been against him going away to fight with SWAPO, however just the cause. Violence was not the way, his father had told him, but he had been young and angry, so he had gone.

Now, with blood on his hands, and having not seen or talked to anyone in his family since leaving for the training bases in southern Angola, how could he face his father and mother? What would his two brothers think of him returning after all these years when they had stayed and worked to help their parents? Perhaps they had families of their own now. They had stayed home in peace and poverty, working the land as best they could and looking to God for guidance. God. God had turned his back on Patrick long ago, he knew. Even Kalunga, the old god of the Owambo, the god who walked among the people when they were in need, had forsaken him when he had gone to Angola. He had walked alone for many years, and it weighed on him.

No, he had had no choice when Tuhadeli had told him he would be going with the American. He had helped Matt load the vehicle when Tuhadeli had introduced them. He had hardly spoken a word in the two days before they had found the carcass of the dead rhino. Matt had tried to make conversation, but Patrick's silence had won out.

What had made him decide to help Matt? He'd been thinking about that. He didn't want to die, though he felt as if he had died many years ago in the war. Tuhadeli must have chosen him because he was dispensable. He knew it was true. His family must have decided he was dead when he didn't return from the war all those years before. The old lady from whom he rented the room wouldn't miss him. He had few enough possessions, and if he were killed, she would take them and rent the room out to someone else. He hadn't been with Tuhadeli long enough for the man to view him as anything other than hired help. No, if he died, no one would note his passing.

Matt did not deserve to die, though. He was a stranger in the country who had come to help. He carried a gun but was not violent. He could have shot the poacher on the hill if he had chosen to, but he hadn't. He had let the man live, although the poacher would have had a thirsty drive home. The memory made Patrick smile. They had done a good thing that day.

Patrick sensed Matt was being used by Tuhadeli. He didn't understand why, but he felt it. Tuhadeli wanted something from Matt, something from the rhinos, but just what wasn't clear to him. The poachers were bad men, and enough evil had been done in this country. So, he would help Matt. Perhaps Kalunga would walk with them in the coming days. The thought gave him a sense of comfort, and he closed his eyes and fell asleep on the roof of the vehicle.

* * *

Matt woke early, before the sun crested the horizon. Patrick was already by the small stove cooking breakfast. Matt went over and sat down next to him, looking into the pot to see what he was making. Canned beef and beans and a pot of coffee.

"I see you are as good a cook as I am," he said.

Patrick stuck a fork into the pot and stirred the beef and beans around. "It was good last night for dinner, so it will also be good this morning for breakfast," he said without looking up.

Matt laughed and reached over to pour himself a mug of coffee. It was strong, but tasted good against the cool morning air.

"What do we do today?" Patrick asked him.

Matt looked at the base of the hill where they were camped.

"After breakfast, let's get to the top of the hill. We'll get a better view of the land from up there."

* * *

Patrick had been right, Matt thought as he climbed the hill. The beef and beans had made a good breakfast. There had been some left in the pot after they had both eaten. Matt had made sure that Patrick finished it. It was good to see him eat. Patrick had stayed with the Rover and was packing up camp. The hill was fairly large, and it took Matt half an hour to get to the top for a panoramic view of the surrounding land. A few plateaued hills dotted the horizon several kilometers away and looked as barren as his current perch. Matt sat down on a large rock to think. It was a vast area of land to cover and a harsh environment. An animal as large as a rhino would have to travel great distances to get water and forage. They could either try to track the animals, or they could wait for the animals to come to them.

He didn't have the resources or time to try to track rhinos in the desert. His best chance of finding one was to locate a regular source of water. It would be like hunting white-tailed deer in Maryland, he thought, without the snow and woods, but the same. All he had to do was find a good place to put his hide and then wait for the animals to come to him. Matt lifted a pair of binoculars and scanned the horizon, searching for any sign of green. Nothing. He panned across the horizon again, picking out a large hill. That was where they would go next. He would climb that hill and look for signs of vegetation or water. The animals were desert adapted, but they still needed to eat and drink. So there would be water. It was just a matter of finding it.

He had come a long way, and he wanted to find a live rhino on this trip. They had plenty of fuel and water, and also a healthy supply of beef and beans, so he didn't think Patrick would mind staying in the field for a few days.

It took them several hours and three hills before Matt found what he was looking for: another seasonal riverbed running through a rugged set of hills. But this one had something different. A small stand of mopane trees hung on next to the riverbed, and behind them was a dense patch of reeds. This time, Patrick had climbed the hill with him. Matt gave him the binoculars and pointed to the distant patch of green.

"What do you think?"

"I think it will be a good place to make camp."

"I think you are right. We'll have to find the source of the water. There must be a natural spring."

It took them another hour to get to the riverbed. Matt stopped the Rover two hundred yards away, as he didn't want to get too close to the reeds. If there were any animals in the area, it wouldn't surprise him to find them sheltering there.

Matt parked on a gentle incline at the base of a hill, overlooking the dried riverbed and the reed bank. From here they had a good view of the small natural spring and the most obvious routes any animals would use to approach it. The heat was intense, and they opened all the windows of the vehicle to get any cross breeze they could. Matt reached into the back seat and grabbed his canteen of water.

"Want some?" he asked as he offered it to Patrick. It had been a long day of driving. Patrick took a long drink before passing the canteen back.

"Well, now we wait."

It was mid-afternoon, and, with the vehicle parked, the heat was oppressive. Matt had his camera on his lap, and Patrick was scanning the reed bank with the binoculars, looking for any sign of movement that would indicate an animal hiding. Three hours passed in sweltering silence without them seeing anything.

"Shall I cook dinner?"

"Not tonight," Matt said, as he viewed his companion. "We'll have to eat straight out of the can. If any animals come, it will probably be from now on into the night. We don't want to scare them off by setting up a camp this close to the water. Best just to sit and wait. Feel free to grab something to eat out of the back though."

"No beef and beans tonight then?" Patrick asked.

"We can have them again, just cold."

That seemed to mollify Patrick somewhat, and he stepped out of the vehicle to get into the back seat so he could reach the supplies. As he started to open the back door, he froze. Matt looked over at him and then glanced through the back window in the direction he was staring.

"Get back in and close the door, but don't slam it," he urged Patrick.

Patrick looked at him and nodded his head, quickly sitting back down and closing the door quietly behind him.

Matt picked up his camera and took a shot through the back window. A lone bull elephant had walked along the base of the hill and was coming across the incline behind them, walking towards the water and the reeds. Patrick sat wide-eyed, looking into the passenger side mirror at the elephant striding closer.

"Just sit tight. He'll probably walk right past us. He's just interested in the water," Matt said, glancing at Patrick, who was frozen, staring at the mirror. From the look on his face, Matt could tell he was not convinced about the elephant's intentions.

The elephant loomed closer, and larger, until its gray mass dominated the back window of the Rover. Then it slowly passed by Patrick's side, pausing for a moment and flapping its large, gray ears.

Patrick sat absolutely still, looking at the elephant in wonder. "Is it angry?" he asked Matt quietly.

"No, it's just cooling itself. Their bodies generate a lot of heat, and flapping their ears helps them lose some of it."

Patrick looked unconvinced, and Matt suppressed a smile.

The elephant stood near them for a few minutes before walking down to quench its thirst at the small spring.

Matt leaned out the window and started to take some photos while Patrick stared at the animal through his binoculars. It wasn't a black rhino, Matt thought, but it was a special moment.

Chapter 8

Silke found her way to the headquarters of Rhinos International on a small back street behind Windhoek's central post office. There, waiting in the lobby for her, was Mphuswe Sithole, the director. She was a large Namibian woman with a welcoming smile. She seemed delighted that the reporter from the *Namibian Star* had come to see her again.

"How can I help you?" she asked Silke, motioning her to a sofa in the reception area after they had greeted each other.

"I'm researching a story on rhinos and need some information," said Silke, coming straight to the point.

"Yes, we've all read your story on the American rhino incident. As you know, we've been studying rhinos for more than thirty years now and have a full archive of reports on everything about them. Just tell me what you need, and I'll get you the reports."

"I'd like to get whatever you have that is up-to-date, but it is the poaching that interests me most."

"Why that?"

"Well, it seems that Namibia is becoming more deeply involved, and we are trying to find out who is behind it."

Mphuswe confirmed that poachers were becoming

increasingly active in parts of Namibia and voiced concerns that her group's efforts to save the rhinos might not be successful. The Namibian police, she lamented, seemed reluctant to get as involved as they should be. "As far as we can tell, it is international. We believe the seed money is coming from Asia. The traditional medicine markets in Southeast Asia are exploding at the moment, and the demand just keeps growing. Years ago, most of the poached horns were going to Yemen for use in traditional dagger handles, but now almost all of them go to Asia for traditional medicine. Unfortunately, the Asians can't seem to get enough rhino horn."

"We want to try to follow the trail and see where it leads us," Silke said.

"You should be careful," cautioned Mphuswe. "It's getting to be a bloody business. We've heard of actual killings, which is frightening in a place as quiet as Namibia. A very bloody business, I tell you. The greater the demand, the higher the price, and the higher the price, the more risks the poachers are willing to take. That's why they have now moved into Namibia. They are prepared to go to any lengths to find rhinos. They have been operating in Etosha and have recently moved into Damaraland."

Mphuswe told Silke that the latest intelligence from the field suggested a major poaching ring was working near Ruacana, on the border with Angola. "You can see how desperate they are if they go there. It is in the middle of nowhere and very difficult to find the rhinos."

"I'll definitely go there then," said Silke, seeing the possibility of a helpful lead. "Do you have a contact in the field who could help me?"

"You're in luck," replied Mphuswe. "We have a young

Norwegian student in Khorixas. He is doing his PhD thesis on rhino conservation in Damaraland. He's been in the field a few weeks now and should have a handle on things up there. His name is Johan Eriksson, and he is staying in a small hotel. I will give him a call and tell him you are coming."

Before Silke left, Mphuswe produced a handful of reports and the contact information for all the authors.

"Thank you so much. I really appreciate it."

"I hope it helps. If you need anything else, let me know."

* * *

The drive to Khorixas took most of the following day. After booking into the hotel, Silke took a quick shower to wash away the dust from the journey. She changed into a silk blouse and a short skirt, the only non-safari clothes she had packed, and then knocked on the door to room 14.

The door was opened by a young blond man with a deep tan and a taut body wearing only his shorts.

"You must be Silke," said Johan, with a slight Scandinavian accent. He extended his hand and laughed. "Excuse me, I'm a bit underdressed. If you hold on a minute, I will put a shirt on, and then we can talk over a drink."

Silke flushed and smiled. "That would be lovely," she said.

* * *

The next day, Johan took her into the field and showed her a female rhino and a calf. He had been tracking the animals for several days. Silke took out her camera and started to take some photographs. She knew photos like these would be perfect for her story. Readers would readily empathize with images of a baby rhino peeking out from between its mother's legs.

On the second day, they went to the scene of a recently poached rhino. Little remained of it other than the skull and rib cage and patches of sun-dried skin. It had been heavily scavenged.

"There's something interesting going on here that we haven't figured out yet."

"What's that?" Silke asked.

"Follow me," Johan said as he walked a short distance away from the carcass and knelt down.

"You see these tracks? Well, it's actually two sets of tracks. The first set, leading away from the carcass, I believe is the poachers. Then another set comes after, intersecting the first set here."

"Really? That is interesting, but how do you know the other tracks came after the first set?"

"The more recent ones had parked their vehicle about a hundred and fifty meters over there and then approached the rhino. They circled the carcass, crossing over the poachers' tracks. And you see here, where they measured out a stride and marked a rough box on the ground?"

"Yes. What's that for?"

"It's a technique used to count how many people you are following. The people who went after the poachers have some bush knowledge and are not your normal tourists for sure."

"So, how many people were there?"

"Well, the first set especially is starting to drift over, but I think there were three poachers, and then two more people tracking the poachers. It's hard to know for sure, but that's what it looks like."

"Where do the tracks lead?"

"I've followed them both. The second set of people followed the poachers' tracks for a while before stopping and going off to the side to climb a hill."

"What do you think was happening?"

"Well, somebody obviously came across the carcass and tracked the poachers for a distance. Why they left the tracks and went up the hill, I don't know. Perhaps they wanted to get up higher to get a better view of where the poachers were going. The poachers' own tracks disappear a couple of kilometers beyond that point. Perhaps they thought they were close to the poachers or suspected a trap. There was a gruesome murder here not too long ago of a local man who had gone into the desert by himself. Very nasty situation that. Apparently, he had been tortured and shot. His body was dumped on the main road in town. I don't think the police have come up with any suspects, though."

"Do you think the police have a role in this?"

"It's hard to say. I don't really know much about what they do, but they don't seem to be too engaged. Now, whether that is because they are understaffed, corrupt or afraid, that's beyond me. Africa can be a crazy place, you know."

*　*　*

Silke thought back to that conversation and the dead rhinos as she drove north towards Ruacana. Now there was a death in Namibia that could possibly be connected to the Damaraland black rhinos. On her way back to Windhoek she would have to stop off in Khorixas again and see if she could find out more about the dead man and why he had gone into the desert. Two murders in America and now one in Namibia in the course of the last month, two slaughtered rhinos, South African military guns and a mystery source for her feature—the story was getting increasingly complex.

The extra tracks at the carcass of the rhino also played on her mind. They could have been made by curious tourists, but then why had they turned away from the tracks and climbed a hill? And what were the chances that tourists in the area would happen to know how to track people and estimate the number of people they were following? *Slim*, she thought. And why would they have tried to track the poachers in the first place? The rhino carcass might have attracted tourists hoping to see other animals. If tourists had figured out that it was killed as a result of poaching, they would have been more likely to report it to the police than to attempt to track the poachers.

The road stretched out ahead of the car, straight and empty. She rolled down her window as she pressed down on the accelerator, and she felt a wave of pleasure wash over her.

Johan was a year or two younger than she was, and he had spent too much time in the bush looking for rhinos. Silke laughed as the car picked up speed. It hadn't taken much to get him to sleep with her, just a few subtle touches on his arm. He had picked up on her cues quickly. The last night in the motel had been liberating. In his enthusiasm, he had been clumsy at first, but she had slowed him down, guided him, brought him into rhythm with her own body. It had been a deeply satisfying final break from her time with Karl. She knew now that when this story was finished, her time in Namibia was over. She was going on to bigger and better things. She was going home.

The car accelerated smoothly on the empty road, and she turned on the CD player. The music blared from the speakers as the wind blew through her hair. It was a good time to be in Africa, she thought.

*   *   *

Matt jotted down some notes on his pad. It was their second evening at the small spring, and a small band of Hartmann's zebra were making their way to the water. Matt knew they were rare and took some photos. Patrick was asleep in the back seat. He had stayed up most of the previous night watching the elephant and keeping an eye out for any rhino that might appear.

The elephant had stayed with them through the morning before going on its way, vanishing silently into the vastness of the desert. Matt had managed to capture some of his best elephant images the previous evening, in the soft desert light. There had been no rhinos, however. He wasn't really expecting them to show themselves in the short time he was in the desert. His notes outlined his basic thoughts on what he would recommend to Reddman when he returned to America.

Genesis Inc. would have to fully engage with the Namibian Ministry of Wildlife Conservation and would need to develop deep partnerships with the various organizations with knowledge of the animals and the land. As for his preliminary assessment of how the project was going, he thought Tuhadeli was a mistake. The man offered no real insight into the desert, its landscape or its fauna. That begged a larger question. Why was Reddman so insistent on using him as the main contact? Matt understood the sensitivities involved with the loss of the rhino in Maryland, but not engaging with the main conservation players in the country was making his preliminary assessment of the area more difficult. If Reddman was serious about his project, he would have to reach out to these groups and overcome whatever mistrust existed.

Matt reached into his pocket and took out the piece of paper that Tuhadeli had given him with the information on the license plate. It was the one bit of real information Tuhadeli had supplied: Pik Malan of Ruacana. The address given with the registration was for a game ranch outside of Ruacana: Sundowner Safaris, a company specializing in evening wildlife drives and trips for tourists to Ruacana Falls.

Tuhadeli had shown him some photos of the falls. He hadn't heard of them before, but the photos showed a dramatic waterfall that was sure to draw a steady, if unspectacular, stream of tourists to the area. Ruacana, on the border with Angola, would definitely be off the main tourist routes through the country, but there would be money to be made.

Matt looked at a map of the country. Ruacana had easy access to Damaraland and also access across the border into southern Angola. It was isolated from the main cities and towns of Namibia. Matt suspected that despite the draw of the waterfalls, Ruacana was an impoverished backwater in the Namibian landscape—and for that reason an ideal place for a criminal group to set up an illegal wildlife operation. The police there were probably extremely provincial in their outlook and easily corrupted.

Matt was also thinking about his next step. He could

just call it a day and return home with his recommendations to Reddman. He had seen the towns and landscape
and already understood many of the difficulties they would
face in setting up an operation. That would be the easy way.
Patrick could return to working odd jobs for Tuhadeli, and
neither of them would be put in harm's way. He folded the
piece of paper back up and stuck it into his pocket.

Pik Malan. Was he really the man on the hill? The man
on the hill had not shown his face from beneath the brim
of his hat, but Matt felt certain he would know him again
if he saw him. Whoever he was, it was clear that he was
dangerous. Slaughtering an animal like the rhino was bad
enough, but to be willing to gun a person down in cold
blood spoke to something else. Matt also thought about the
other man, the man whose body had been thrown onto
the road in Khorixas after being tortured. If it were the
poachers who had killed him, it was clear that violence came
easily to them. Matt had pressed Tuhadeli for information
on 32 Battalion. Patrick had told him about the Buffalos'
reputation from the war of independence. The story in the
Namibian Star about the South African connection to the
Maryland incident also played across his mind. Was there
a connection between the two? Why would a poaching
ring in Africa go after a rhino in America?

Patrick stirred in the back seat and sat up, wiping the
sleep from his eyes. "Did the elephant come back?" he
asked Matt as he looked out the window and tried to focus.

"No, I think he has gone for a long walk. It might be
some time before he comes back," Matt replied.

"Are we going to stay here and wait for a rhino?"

"Well, it is already early evening, so we will stay one
more night and see if our luck changes. In the morning,

we will drive back to the main road and head towards Ruacana to see what we can find out about these poachers. What do you think?"

Patrick looked at him for a moment. "I think that is a good idea."

Chapter 9

The police captain glared at Silke across his desk. "Why would you ask me such a question? We have no poaching here of our wildlife."

The interview was not going well. The man had been suspicious and defensive from the start. Silke had tried to put him at ease, but was making little headway and was getting increasingly annoyed.

"I have just come from Damaraland, where I have seen the carcass of a rhino that was recently poached. It is from the same population of rhinos as the animal that was recently slaughtered in America," she said.

"How do you know this rhino was poached, and why do you come here to ask me about it? You should ask the police in Okatjuru or Opuwo. Maybe they know something for you. Why have you come here?"

Silke had conducted a number of hostile interviews before, usually with local politicians who were being investigated for corruption. The more hostile they were, the deeper the guilt was her rule of thumb. "Well, I've talked to rhino experts in the field who are studying the population in Damaraland, and they think a poaching ring is located near Ruacana. I've also had information that there may be a South African connection, both to the poaching here and to the recent incident in America. Do you know anything about that?"

"I told you, there are no poachers in Ruacana and no South Africans."

"What about a recent murder in Khorixas? The body was left in the main street. Apparently the man had been tortured before he was shot. It is thought the man might have gone into Damaraland to track the poachers." She hadn't intended to bring up the murder, but she was getting increasingly angry with the man, and it slipped out.

"I have told you, there is no poaching here, and I know nothing of a murder in Khorixas. The interview is over." The man stood up. "You journalists ask too many questions. We do not forget what you write. Remember that."

On her way to the door, Silke stopped for a moment. The captain was a big man, and he loomed over her. There was a menace in his tone. "Are you threatening me?" she asked, meeting his gaze. She might have been intimidated a few years earlier, but she was damned if a small town policeman was going to get away with a thinly veiled threat.

"I am just saying that we have a good memory when we see stories printed in the newspaper."

"I will continue my investigation with or without your help, you realize, and I will run the story as it presents itself. Thank you for your time," Silke said, flushing and stalking out the door. Despite herself, she was frustrated with the exchange. She had hoped the police might have some useful leads, but instead, the man had been defensive and abrupt.

Driving back to the small lodge she had booked into, she considered the interview. He must know something, she thought, or perhaps be involved. Why be so hostile otherwise? Before returning to her bungalow, she stopped off in the lodge's bar to get a drink and to re-read her background notes on the rhinos.

On the face of it, the interview had gone badly, but it had been telling. If no poaching group was in the area, why was the policeman so belligerent? It would have been easy for him to answer a few questions, but he hadn't. Did that really mean anything, though? The *Namibian Star* and its reporters had a reputation of going after corrupt officials. A local police captain who wasn't used to being questioned by a journalist might overreact when put on the spot.

Perhaps it was me, she thought. *Perhaps he has seen the recent stories in the* Namibian Star *and is worried about appearing in the paper.* A man like that can't have had too much experience with the press. Perhaps his defensiveness was a result of her recent story. But he had ended the interview with an implied threat. *Don't they put the police through any media training when they promote them?*

"Can I get you something?"

Silke looked up. It was the bartender. He appeared to be in his fifties, with short gray hair and a weathered face. He was wearing a neat white coat with the logo of the lodge over his left pocket. She guessed he was an Owambo.

"Do you have a decent Chardonnay?"

The bartender smiled. "We have several. Would you like to try something from the Cape?"

The South African Cape—the mention of home made the trouble with the police captain seem silly. She should have approached the whole interview differently. She tried to put herself in the police captain's shoes. In such a remote and lightly populated area, he probably didn't deal with much crime at all. To be confronted by a reporter from the nation's leading newspaper would be a bit intimidating, and a woman reporter at that. The more she thought about it, the more reasonable the man's defensiveness appeared.

"A glass of Chardonnay from the Cape would be wonderful."

She took a deep sip from the glass, letting the wine cascade across her tongue before slowly swallowing it. "That is good. You may need to get me another glass before too long."

The bartender smiled. "That is what I am here for, and as you can see, business is a bit slow today."

The bar was empty, not that she minded. It had been a long drive up to Ruacana, and her first interview had not gone as expected. That could be recovered, she thought. She would give it a day or two and approach the police captain again, but this time in a more conciliatory frame of mind. She would put him more at ease, soften him up a bit. The man would come around, she was sure.

"So, are you in town to see the waterfalls?" the bartender asked as he cleaned a glass.

"No. Actually, I'm a reporter for the *Namibian Star*. I'm here doing a follow-up story on the Damaraland rhinos. It's about poaching the rhinos for their horn. I just interviewed the local police captain. I'm afraid that didn't go too well."

The bartender gave a short laugh. "It is difficult to deal with that man. I remember when we were children at school. He was a bully then, and he still is one now. I am surprised that he talked to you at all. My name is Lazrus, by the way."

Silke picked up her glass and took another sip of the wine. It really was good. Ruacana was a small town, she realized, a town where everyone probably knew each other's business.

"Well, I will try with the mayor tomorrow and then perhaps with your friend from school again in a day or so. My name is Silke."

The bartender was silent for a moment, still wiping the already clean glass. "You won't get much out of the mayor or the police, I suspect. Would you like to talk to some of the local people who might have an idea of what is happening?"

"That would be really helpful. Can you help me set that up?"

"If you don't mind going to one of the shabeens in town, I can get a friend to take you in and introduce you to some of the people. You won't be able to get a nice Cape wine, but perhaps something with more of a local flavor."

Later that evening, Silke returned to the bar. There was a young couple in khaki shorts, sandals and T-shirts sitting at the far end of the bar enjoying a drink and some food. The bartender came over as she sat down.

"My friend will be here shortly to take you to the #1 Gangster Bar. It is one of the more popular shabeens in town. Do you mind if the young couple over there goes with you? They are looking to get a taste of the local nightlife."

Silke looked at the couple at the far end of the bar and smiled. It might put anyone she talked to at ease if she was in a group.

"Sure. They'd be most welcome. The more, the merrier."

It turned out Luca and Sofie were from Germany. They were visiting relatives in the coastal town of Swakopmund and had traveled north to Ruacana to see the falls. This was their final night in town.

The bartender's friend showed up as the three of them started to chat. He was a tall young man wearing a Kaiser Chiefs baseball cap.

"This is Shilli," the bartender introduced him.

"Are you ready for a night at the Gangster?" Shilli said, flashing a broad, friendly grin. He looked at the young couple and added, "It has the best music and beer in Ruacana!"

"We are ready and waiting," Luca said and stood up to shake Shilli's hand.

Shilli looked at Silke and shook her hand as she offered it. "And you must be the newspaper lady who has annoyed our town's friendly policeman." He laughed. "We will see if we can find you someone else to talk to, but you must be nice to them!"

Silke laughed. "I was nice to him. I think he just got up on the wrong side of the bed this morning!"

Shilli walked them out to his van. It was dark blue and dusty from the local dirt roads, and the front windows didn't close. Luca and Sofie piled into the back seat, leaving Silke to sit up front with Shilli.

"So, what do you do, Shilli?" Silke asked as they drove away from the lodge and turned towards town.

"I do many things. Tonight I am your Go-Faster taxi service."

"Perhaps for tonight, you could be our Get-There-Slowly-and-Safely taxi service," Sofie chimed in from the back seat, and they all laughed.

"If I go slowly, I will have less time with all the fine ladies tonight. They may not be happy with you!"

The drive from the lodge to the #1 Gangster Bar took about ten minutes. Shilli pulled the van up in front of an unremarkable one-story cinderblock building that had been painted orange. Across the top of the building, in bright red paint, was "#1 Gangster Bar." The front was lit by a single lightbulb that was powered by a wire that had been run through one of the two front windows. A typical shabeen, Silke thought.

"Not exactly like a night club in Munich, I daresay." Silke smiled at Luca and Sofie.

"No, not at all. I think this will be better," Luca said, getting out of the car.

Inside, the lighting wasn't much better. A single lightbulb was hanging from a wire in the center of the ceiling, but the room was packed with people drinking home-brewed beer from plastic containers. Some music blared from a CD player plugged into the back wall. When they first walked in, the group got a few cold stares, and a couple dancing in the middle of the room stopped for a moment, but when Shilli walked in behind the others, the mood lightened quickly.

Shilli raised his hand and indicated four drinks from a young man towards the back of the room.

"Come. There is a table over here."

It was little more than an old garden table with four old chairs around it, but it served the purpose. The drinks arrived, and Shilli passed them around. Silke paid.

"These are on me." She smiled at Shilli.

After a quick drink, Luca pulled Sofie up to join the other people dancing.

As they stood up, a middle-aged man with bloodshot eyes came over and sat down. Shilli introduced him to Silke. "This is Martin. I will leave you to talk. My lady friends are waiting for me to join them."

Silke raised her hand to indicate she wanted another drink for Martin.

"You know who I am?" she asked.

"Yes, you are the newspaper lady from Windhoek. You want to know about rhinos."

Silke smiled. The bartender and Shilli had obviously briefed him. "Yes, that is right. Do you know anything?"

Martin's beer arrived, and he took a deep swallow. Silke touched her lips to her own beer, but she was careful not to drink much. She had visited shabeens before and enjoyed their atmosphere, but she had never acquired a taste for the home-brewed beers that were popular in them.

"I do. I have worked on many farms and ranches near town." Martin leaned back and took another deep mouthful of the beer. He was enjoying being the center of attention. "My last job was with Sundowner Safaris."

"Do they have a game ranch?" Silke asked.

"Yes. Like most farms, they have cattle, but also game. Mostly kudu, gemsbok and a few zebra. There is a leopard and a few cheetah as well, but they are difficult to find."

"Do they have any rhinos?"

"Not as far as I know. Rhinos are hard to find."

He wiped some of the beer off his chin as he finished his drink. He put the container back down on the table and looked at it and then at Silke. Silke smiled, picked the container up and went to get him another drink. He smiled as she sat back down and gave him the drink.

"You would make a good wife," Martin said. "My wife now doesn't like me to come here. I have to sneak away while she isn't looking. She thinks I have another woman."

Silke laughed. "If I was your wife, I would not have any money left. You drink as if this were your last day!" She grew more serious. "But why are you telling me about this ranch?"

"They are strange people that run the ranch. I was there for one year, and while they don't have many tourists come, they have their own runway for small planes."

"That is not unusual for a game ranch," Silke interjected. "A lot of people fly small planes here. It's an easy way to get around the country."

"Yes, it is not unusual to have a runway on a farm, but at Sundowner, they got very angry if they found you near it. I did odd jobs around the farm, but they made it clear we were to stay away from the runway and the building there."

"Why did you leave?" Silke asked. Any job in Ruacana must be hard to come by, and she wondered if Martin was just a disgruntled worker who wanted to cause a hassle for his ex-employers.

"Pik Malan, he was why I left."

"Who is Pik Malan?"

"He owns the ranch. One day, he beat one of the farm workers when he didn't notice a new calf had been taken by a leopard. He put the man in hospital. There had been nothing that could have been done for the calf. The man just didn't see that it had been taken. So Malan beat him."

"Didn't the police do anything?"

"The police? The police here do not care. Malan is too important in the town, and he is friends with the police. He always makes sure they are taken care of, so they look the other way and do nothing. I do not know if the ranch has anything to do with poaching, but I would not be surprised. Pik Malan was always taking trips away from the ranch, and it was never said where he was going on these trips."

Pik Malan. She would have to ask the mayor about him tomorrow. The violence that Martin described didn't bother

her as much as the attitude about the airstrip. Violence was a regular part of life at many farms. Old animosities ran deep in rural Africa.

"Thank you, Martin. I'll see what I can find out about Sundowner and Pik Malan."

She bought him another beer, as he had quickly downed the previous one. "Just don't tell your wife I bought it for you." She smiled as he got up.

Shilli, true to his word, was standing in the corner with two young women. Luca and Sofie were still dancing, but they had swapped partners and were obviously enjoying their evening out with the locals. Silke leaned back in her chair and took a sip of the beer.

It was past midnight when they started to make their way back to the lodge. Shilli, despite all the attention from the women, had managed not to drink much.

"It is like that every time I go to the Gangster, but I must get up early tomorrow and work," he said as they got back into the van.

Luca and Sofie collapsed in the back seat. They had hardly sat down all night. It was a quiet drive back to the lodge. Silke didn't mind the window being stuck down, as the cool breeze washed through the vehicle. Shilli dropped them off at the lodge and said good night, driving off into the darkness.

Silke walked with Luca and Sofie for a short distance.

"Good night," she said as they parted ways. "My bungalow is on the other side of the camp."

Silke walked slowly back towards her bungalow. After several hours in the crowded, noisy shabeen, she was enjoying the quiet and dark of the African night. It had been a good night. She wasn't sure that Martin had provided much of a lead for her story, but time would tell. Her interview with the mayor the following morning might also yield more light. She walked around the corner of an empty bungalow.

She caught a movement out of the corner of her eye and turned around. A man was behind her. She could see his face clearly in the moonlight. It was the police captain. She opened her mouth to say something, but he moved too quickly. She didn't make a sound as his fist crashed into the side of her head. She staggered back a step, but managed to stay on her feet. She again tried to say something, but the words just wouldn't come. She saw the second blow coming and tried to raise her hand to protect herself, but she seemed to be moving in slow motion. She saw a brief flash of light as his fist crashed into her temple, and then she collapsed unconscious to the ground.

Chapter 10

Matt and Patrick stopped briefly in Ruacana to refuel and to buy some supplies and then booked into a small campsite a few miles outside of town. The campsite was next to a lodge, but they both preferred the isolation offered by the camp.

"It's still early afternoon," Matt said, looking up at the sky. "We'll have time to take a quick look around before dark."

They got back into the Land Rover and followed the main road until a small sign directed them to turn down a dirt side road. A game fence ran along the road about fifteen yards back. After about five miles, they came to a nondescript gate with a weather-worn sign that announced "Sundowner Safaris." Beside the gate was a small guardhouse that looked like it was occupied. Without slowing, Matt drove past the entrance. He kept going for a number of miles before pulling over to the side of the road.

"What do you think?" Matt asked Patrick. There had been only the one entrance along the ten miles of road they had driven since leaving the main road.

"I think we should wait here a while before driving back. We don't want to bring too much attention to ourselves by driving up and down the road. The guard was probably asleep, but you never know. He might have noticed us drive by."

"Yeah, that's a good point."

"Tomorrow you should drive me to where this road meets the main road, and I will walk along the fence until I find a good place to go through. I will scout the ranch and see if there is anything to find," said Patrick.

Matt thought for a moment. He had gained an appreciation for Patrick's bush craft and had little doubt he could handle himself in a hostile area. "Agreed. While you're doing that, I'll go into town and see if I can find out anything there. How long do you think you'll need?"

"Well, it is a big ranch, but once I come across the entrance road, it should be easy to find the main building and facilities. You should drop me off before the sun rises and pick me up at ten at night. That should give me plenty of time to find out if there is anything interesting."

"You're not worried about being seen on the road alone?"

"Do not worry about me. Once I am on the farm, I will be like a ghost in the bush. No one will notice me. And if someone does see me on the side of the road, they will not look twice. There are always people on the side of the road. Better that it is a black man alone than a black man with a white man. That would make someone think there was something strange happening."

They settled on the plan and then waited about an hour before driving back past the entrance to Sundowner. There was no movement in the small guardhouse as they roared past, leaving a cloud of dust in their wake.

* * *

It was still dark the next morning as Patrick started to jog along the side of the game fence. He carried a small backpack with binoculars and some water and biltong to get through the day. He didn't go through the fence right away, as he wanted to get closer to the entrance to Sundowner before moving onto the farm's property. The key to finding the facilities was the access road. He stayed along the fence line, away from the road. It was unlikely anyone would notice his footprints, but he didn't want to take the chance.

He breathed in the cool morning air in a steady rhythm as he jogged, slowly picking up his pace as he went. He ran without shoes, the soles of his feet hardened by a lifetime of going barefoot. This would be a dangerous day. He had seen the body of the man who had gone into Damaraland to track the poachers. He knew these people were capable of violence. Matt had come very close to death that day at the carcass. If he had walked another twenty yards, the man on the hill would have seen him and would have had a clear shot. These were bad people. If he was caught, he could expect a severe beating as a suspected poacher, possibly much worse. It was fairly common for the local people to supplement their diets with poached animals. He and his SWAPO comrades had often taken wild game. For some, it even offered a minor source of income, as they could sell the meat in local markets. The farmers, however, didn't take kindly to the game they had purchased and raised to attract tourists being hunted by non-paying locals looking to make a quick dollar or to fill their bellies.

He had gone about four miles along the road when he heard the sound of an engine. Quickly finding a patch of dried grass near a large bush, he lay down and stayed motionless. It was still dark, but the sun was just beginning to crest the horizon, turning the sky a faded shade of yellow. It took a few minutes before the headlights lurched into sight. Patrick didn't move as they drew closer. The headlights flashed across the long grass and bush where he was hiding as the vehicle came around a turn in the road, but the sound of the engine stayed constant, and the small truck kept going.

Probably a truck from one of the farms on the road heading into town to carry out some business. Everyone is up early today, he thought. The Sundowner property line ran for several miles, but there would be other farms and ranches further down the road.

He waited until the sound of the engine had faded away and then got up and went on. His senses were alive. He hadn't felt like this since the war years when he had played a dangerous game of cat and mouse with the South African Defense Forces. If the people at Sundowner were ex-members of 32 Battalion, he would be dealing with an old and dangerous enemy.

He picked up his jog again, quickly falling into an easy stride. By the time the sun had cleared the horizon and the air was starting to warm, he was within a quarter mile of the entrance gate.

He stopped, opened the small backpack Matt had given him, took out one of the bottles of water and took a quick drink. As he was running, he had noticed the fence was not well maintained, and it didn't take him long to find an area dug under by a warthog. It wasn't a very big hole, but after he slid his pack under the fence, he was able to get through easily enough. He picked his pack up and moved swiftly through the bush, keeping an eye out for any movement. The previous day, when they had driven by the entrance, he'd noticed a large kopje that rose above the bushland about a mile in from the fence. It wasn't far from the access road. If he could get to the top of it, it should provide a good view of the farm and the facilities.

It didn't take him long to find the access road. The sound of another vehicle gave it away. As soon as he heard the engine, he dropped to the ground again. He was still a distance away and could not see the vehicle, but the stakes were too high to be careless. As the engine faded into the distance, Patrick made his way towards the road. The road was packed dirt and provided a break in the bushland that allowed him to see the kopje. He was about half a mile away now. He quickly scanned the road to make sure everything was clear and then made his way across, vanishing on the other side.

The kopje was large, and once he was on top, it provided Patrick with a clear view of the farm and its facilities. The main building was another mile up the access road. It was a large, two-story building with a shaded veranda that ran across the front. Beyond the building was a maintenance yard with several parked vehicles. A lone man walked across the yard, past the vehicles and into a large shed. Across the access road, and about a mile away from the building, there was what looked like a runway, with a small corrugated iron building that Patrick took to be a small hangar. The runway looked like it was packed dirt that had been cleared of brush. It was long enough to accommodate a small plane.

Patrick slipped down the back side of the kopje to think. If they were running a poaching operation, they wouldn't keep any evidence of it at the main building, where they might have tourists and other guests. He hadn't seen any activity at the runway, and, unless a plane was flying in, Patrick suspected it would remain deserted. He would make a quick reconnaissance of the airstrip and see if he could find anything in the hangar. Then he would make his way back to the kopje and keep a watch on the house.

It only took about twenty minutes for him to get to the airstrip. The back of the building was made of corrugated iron except for two windows and a wooden door. He scanned the outside of the building and the road leading to the airstrip. There was no movement or sound.

Moving quickly, he approached the back of the building and looked through one of the windows. Along the back wall there were some crates loosely covered by a tarp, as well as a worktable. A couple of old, metal-framed chairs were against one of the side walls, and some fuel barrels were stacked against the other. In the center was a space large enough to hold a small plane, and most of the front wall was taken up by a set of hangar doors. There was nobody inside the building. He went to the door at the back and turned the handle. It was unlocked. Taking a quick look behind him, he entered the hangar.

He went immediately to the crates and pulled the tarp back. The top box was unsealed, and he slid the top off to see what was inside. It was what he was looking for: packed with old newspapers, there were four cut rhino horns. The poachers were obviously getting ready to ship them out of the area. He put the packing back in place, closed the lid to the crate and pulled the tarp back over the top.

Just then, he heard the sound of a car door slamming.

Damn, he thought. *The engine sound must have been muffled by the walls of the hangar.* He walked quickly to the back door and opened it just enough to slip through. As he closed it, he heard the hangar doors being pulled back and muffled voices from inside. He ducked below the level of the window and moved to the corner of the building. He wanted to hear what they were saying, but if they came out the back door, he needed to be able to slip out of sight quickly.

The voices drew closer.

"Can you believe that stupid policeman, hey? He panics at the first sign of a reporter, knocks her out and brings her here. Pik is going to go mad when he finds out."

"Ja, he is going to be very angry."

"What should we do with her? She's regained consciousness but is still pretty dazed. He must have hit her very hard."

"I don't give a shit how hard he hit the bitch. Bring her in here, tie her to one of those chairs and leave her here until Pik gets back from Damaraland. He called last night and said he'll be back tomorrow morning. They've taken two more rhinos—one in Etosha and another in Damaraland. Make sure she is gagged and has a hood over her head."

"You got it, boss."

"And make sure this place is locked up tight. Check that back door, will you? Edward is always leaving it unlocked. He hasn't got a clue how much we have at stake here. The plane is flying in tomorrow at noon for the package. We will add the four horns Pik brings in tomorrow to the four already here and then seal up the crate for shipment."

Patrick, hearing the door handle turn, slipped around the corner of the building.

"See what I mean? The door is unlocked. We are going to have to get rid of Edward. He is far too careless."

The door closed again, and he heard the lock click.

"You got some duct tape here? We can use it to tape the woman's arms and legs to the chair and tape her mouth shut. She won't be going anywhere."

"Ja, over there on the workbench there should be a couple of rolls. I wouldn't want to be her when Pik gets back. He's going to want information, and he'll mess her up pretty bad to get it."

"Then what?"

"What do you think? A bullet to the back of the head and a shallow grave out in the bush. Pik doesn't mess around with shit like this. What else can we do? She's a reporter. We can't let her go, or we are all finished."

Patrick stood listening. He was going to have to get Matt out here this evening. A reporter? Had he heard that correctly? They had kidnapped a reporter and were planning on killing her the next day. The rhino horns seemed suddenly insignificant. They were talking about murder.

Eventually, he heard the hangar doors sliding shut and the sound of two car doors closing. He waited a few minutes until the sound of the car engine had faded in the distance, and then he carefully walked around the back of the hanger and peered in through one of the windows. It was much like he had left it a few minutes earlier except for a figure slumped over in one of the chairs with a cloth sack over its head. The arms and legs were taped to the chair.

Patrick started for the door and then stopped himself. It was still early in the day, and he wasn't going to see Matt again until that evening. If he tried to rescue the woman now, he would risk raising the alarm. She was obviously hurt, so he might need Matt's help to move her.

Best to follow the plan, he thought. If the men who had

been in the hangar were right, Malan wasn't returning until the following morning. That would give him time to get Matt and return that night.

He looked through the window one last time and whispered softly, "Do not worry. I will see you tonight."

He carefully retraced his tracks around the building and hid any evidence of his being there. He then walked into the bush, making his way back to the kopje.

Chapter 11

I should have gone with Patrick, Matt thought. *A whole day wasted in Ruacana, and nothing learned.* He had parked the Rover a distance off the main road so any people passing wouldn't see it. He glanced at his watch. He was early, but he wanted to make sure Patrick didn't have to wait for him.

Suddenly, out of the dark, he saw a figure dart across the main road and head for the vehicle. He leaned over and unlocked the passenger door just as Patrick arrived and got into the truck.

"We must go back to the ranch now," Patrick said, almost breathless. "They are going to kill a woman in the morning, and we must get her out."

"How do you know this?" Matt asked, stunned.

"I overheard them say it, and I saw the woman tied to a chair. I believe it is a journalist. They also have a crate with four rhino horns that they are getting ready to fly out tomorrow."

"You saw that as well?"

"Yes, and they are bringing in more horns tomorrow for a plane that is coming later in the day. They have killed two more rhinos—one in Etosha and another in Damaraland."

"The one from Damaraland is probably the one we saw."

Patrick nodded. He was sweating and seemed tired. Matt passed him some water. He leaned back and thought a moment as Patrick took a deep drink.

"How was the woman? Has she been hurt?"

"She did not look well. Apparently she had been hit very hard in the head. They said a policeman had done it."

That could complicate things, Matt thought. Out loud, he said, "We will have to get the Rover closer to the ranch entrance then. If the woman has been hurt, it will be difficult to carry her all this distance."

"Yes, we can drive along the road for a while and then pull off into the bush on the opposite side of the road. There are a couple of places where we can hide the vehicle so we won't have to travel too far on foot. Hopefully, she can walk by herself, or it will be difficult."

"We will also want to get the rhino horns. That will be the proof the police will need to shut these people down." Matt got out of the Rover, pulled out a large sports bag he used when traveling and emptied it. "We can use this for the horns." He grabbed some more water and passed it to Patrick. "That's for the woman we are going to help." He then pulled his hunting rifle out the back, got back into the driver's seat and turned on the engine. "We'll drive in with the headlights off. No need to risk being seen. Do you think you can find the spot where we can hide the vehicle in the dark?"

Patrick nodded his head. "That will not be a problem." He paused. "I do not think these people are South African soldiers," he added.

"Why do you say that?"

"They are not very careful. They leave doors unlocked, and it did not take me very long to find the horns. They were in the first place I looked. They also have this person, and although they tied her to a chair, they did not leave a guard with her. These are bad people, but they are not soldiers."

"That's good to know, but we have to be very careful here. Soldiers or not, they are willing to kill."

Matt turned on the engine and put the Rover into gear. It powered steadily through the bush, up the incline, across the main road and onto the dirt road.

*   *   *

Silke opened her eyes but could not see anything. The side of her head ached, and she tried to raise her hand to touch it, but couldn't. Her right arm was stuck in place, by her side. She tried to move her other hand, but that, too, was restrained.

What's going on here? she thought. *Where am I, and why can't I move?* She tried to say something, to call out for help, but her lips stayed shut. She tried to stand up, but, like her arms, her legs were strapped tightly to whatever she was sitting on. She started to struggle against the bonds that were holding her, but nothing gave way. Each time she pulled against her restraints, she realized it wasn't just her head that ached; her whole body hurt.

A bead of sweat trickled down her forehead, and she felt a rising sense of panic. She threw all her strength into freeing herself, into trying to move, but again nothing gave.

Calm down and think. What has happened to me? She slowed her breathing. She wanted to open her mouth and breathe in big gulps of fresh air, but she couldn't. The air was thick and claustrophobic. She tried to shake off whatever was covering her head, but it remained in place. She sat still for a few minutes. *Think, Silke, think.*

The previous night slowly came back to her: the night out with Shilli, Luca and Sofie at the Gangster, the talk with Martin, the drive home, the walk back to her bungalow… and then she remembered his face. The police captain. *Oh God, don't let this be happening.* The panic returned, and she threw herself against her bonds. She pulled with her right arm with all her strength and threw her body to the left. If she could just free her right hand, she would be able to release the other restraints. She felt the chair lift, lean to the left and start to fall over. She tried to shift her balance back to stay upright but couldn't stop the momentum of the chair as it crashed to the ground. Her right hand was still strapped tightly to the armrest.

There's nothing I can do, she realized as she lay there. *I can't get away.*

She closed her eyes and tried to think. *What do they want with me?* The police captain knew who she was and what story she was investigating. *I should have been more careful. I should have known he was involved from his reaction to the interview.*

Her head was throbbing with pain, and she was exhausted from the struggle to free herself. She lay, stuck in the chair, for what seemed like an eternity, unable to do anything. As the time passed, she felt herself slipping off to sleep, only to awaken whenever she heard anything. Hours later, or it could have been minutes—she realized she had lost all sense of time—she heard the grating sound of metal doors being pulled back.

"Look. The bitch has toppled over," a voice rang out. "She must have tried to get loose."

Silke lifted her head to try to get an idea of where the voice had come from.

"Look. She's awake now," the voice said again, closer now.

Silke tried to say something, but again couldn't manage to speak through the tape over her mouth.

She felt a sharp pain as a boot flew into her stomach. She groaned. She wanted to double over, to wrap her arms around her waist, but she couldn't move.

"That's for trying to get loose and tipping the chair over," the voice said. "Now you need to behave yourself, understand?"

Silke tried to say yes, but nothing came out.

The man struck her on the head, and a bolt of pain shot through her.

"Just nod your head if you understand."

Silke nodded.

Rough hands grabbed her then and jerked the chair back onto its legs. She went rigid, steeling herself for another blow. When none came, she relaxed a little and let her head sag forward. *Please let this end,* she thought.

"Ed, double-check the horns, and also make sure she hasn't managed to get any of that tape loose. We don't want her causing any trouble tonight."

"You got it, boss."

"And just to make sure, you're going to stay here overnight, so you better find a place to make yourself comfortable."

"Are you serious? We are in the middle of nowhere. What the hell can happen here?"

"Don't give me any of your shit, Ed. Tomorrow is too important. You realize who that lady is, don't you? That stupid policeman has kidnapped a newspaper reporter with the *Namibian Star*, and now we are going to have to deal with it. The stakes are a whole lot higher now. Pik will sort it out tomorrow when he gets here, but until then I want things nice and quiet. Got it?"

"Yeah, I got it," Ed said sullenly.

Silke heard footsteps walking away, and everything was quiet for a few moments. She then heard a car door slam, an engine start and tires rolling away. A few more minutes of silence passed. She raised her head to see if she could hear anything. *They've gone away,* she thought and breathed a little easier.

Then she smelled it: cigarette smoke. At first, it was just a faint wisp, but then it grew stronger until it was all she could smell. She tried to turn her head away, but a hand clasped her around the chin and turned her face forward again. *How did he move so quietly? I didn't hear a thing.*

"It's just you and me now, bitch, and I think we'll have some fun tonight. I'll be damned if I'm staying here all night just watching you."

A puff of smoke blew through the sack cloth, and Silke started to cough against the acrid smoke.

"Don't like the smoke, hey," Ed said. "Well, I think that will be the least of your worries."

She felt a rough hand reach inside her blouse and rub over her breasts. She flinched at his touch, but she couldn't avoid it.

"Yes," he said. "This is going to be a long night. I hope you enjoy it as much as I will."

Ed took his hand away and walked away. She heard him unlock a door and step outside. "Don't go anywhere, darling. I'll be right back." The door closed behind him.

Don't let this be happening. This can't be happening. I've got to get away while he's not here. Again she struggled against the tape, but if anything it was tighter than before. *I've got to get away from here,* her mind screamed.

After a few minutes, she sagged forward, coated in sweat, exhausted, defeated. Her head throbbed with pain, and her whole body ached. It was futile. She couldn't even get out of the chair.

She heard the door handle turn, and then the door creaked. She started to lift her head to hear any footsteps, but what did it matter? She knew she couldn't do anything about it anyway. That's when she felt the man's hand slide inside her blouse again and again trace an arc around one of her breasts. His hands were large and coarse. The hand moved from her breasts and up to the nape of her neck before slowly encircling her throat. She could hear his ragged breathing. His head must have been right next to hers. The hand gripped harder, large, strong fingers digging deep into her neck. She felt herself struggling for breath. And then she was free, as he released his grip on her neck and threw her and the chair over backwards. She felt a brief moment of weightlessness before she hit the hard dirt floor. Her head snapped back, and pain exploded in her head.

* * *

Ed looked down at the woman. She was still breathing, but there was no other movement. He smiled to himself.

"Now you won't struggle. I hate it when you struggle. Do you hear me?"

It had been a long time since he'd been with a woman, and she hadn't been nearly as compliant as this one was going to be. No one would be the wiser. They had left him here all night to watch her. And for what? They were in the middle of nowhere. Who the hell was going to find her? They were going to kill her in the morning anyway.

He reached around his back and took out his hunting knife. He knelt down next to the woman, cut the tape around her legs and arms and lifted her out of the chair, laying her on the dirt floor. He then tore her blouse open, before cutting the belt to her shorts and pulling those down.

He stood up and admired his work. He had started to unbuckle his own belt when he heard a slight sound behind him. As he turned his head, he caught sight of a rifle stock just before it crashed into his temple, crushing the bone between his right eye and ear. He collapsed to the ground unconscious. He didn't feel the next blow, the one that killed him.

* * *

Patrick leapt forward to pull Matt away from the body of the man. Matt's ferocity had taken him by surprise.

"Did you see what he was going to do? Do you see what he's done to her already?"

"Yes, but it is finished now. And we have a lot of work to do before the night is over if we are to get her away."

Matt took a deep breath and looked down at the man. A pool of blood was slowly expanding around his head.

Patrick was kneeling down next to the woman. He had removed the sack from her head and was pulling the tape away from her mouth. "She's still alive."

Matt knelt down next to her as well and looked at her face. It was swollen and badly bruised, and her breathing was shallow but regular. "They've beaten her up pretty bad. She probably has a nasty concussion at the least. We need to get her back to the Land Rover and then to a hospital."

"I will carry her," Patrick offered.

"Are you sure you can manage?"

Patrick just nodded, a grim look on his face. He gently pulled her clothes back into place, fastening them with pieces of tape.

"Take her now then, and be careful with her head and neck. I will follow you after I have sorted things out here. Where were the horns?"

"In the top crate under the tarp," Patrick said pointing.

Matt helped lift Silke up so Patrick could carry her.

"You keep the pack with the water in case she comes to. I'll follow you quickly. When you get back to the Rover, give me half an hour. If I'm not there by then, leave without me."

Patrick walked out the back door, Silke limp in his arms.

Matt watched them go and then turned back towards the man on the floor. He knelt down and checked for a pulse. There was none. *Damn! He's dead*, he thought. *I've killed the man*. A moment of nausea swept over him. He took a couple of breaths. *Think, man, think. What do you do next?*

Slowly the nausea passed. He got up, walked over to the tarp and pulled it back. Opening the top box, he saw the horns Patrick had described. *Two more rhino dead, but this is coming to an end*. He pulled the horns out one by one and placed them in the sports bag. He then placed the bag by the back door with his rifle.

He looked around the building. The man's body lay limp on the ground next to the chair in which the woman had been taped. On the other side of the hangar were the barrels of fuel.

Matt stood up and walked to the back door to get some fresh air and to think. *We need to cover our tracks, throw this group off our trail.* He looked back at the body, and then at the fuel cans.

He walked back and with an effort lifted the body into the chair. He looked around, found the same duct tape that had been used to tie the lady down and strapped the dead body tightly to the chair. He had seen the cigarette butts and checked the man's pockets. He pulled out a lighter.

Matt then went over to the barrels. On top of them were a couple of gallon jerry cans of fuel. Choosing one and unscrewing the cap, he poured fuel over the body, the tarps and the crates and then made a trail of fuel leading to the barrels. Just to be sure, he got a tool from the worktable and jabbed holes in some of the barrels.

"That should do it," he muttered to himself. Finally, he took the second jerry can and poured a trail of fuel to the back door. He slung the sports bag over his back and picked up his rifle. He took one last look through the door, threw the now empty can back inside the hangar, bent down and lit the fuel. He watched for a second as the fire shot along the dirt floor toward the chair and engulfed the body in a rising column of flame. He then turned away and ran into the darkness after Patrick.

Chapter 12

Matt pulled the camera out of his bag and turned on the display screen. He scrolled through the pictures until he got to the ones of the rhino poaching in Damaraland and handed the camera to Detective Silas Kabali of the Swakopmund police force.

"These are from a poached rhino carcass we came across when we first went into Damaraland," Matt said. "If you scroll past the pictures of the dead rhino, you will come to several of a man on a hill with a hunting rifle, and then some of his vehicle."

"And these are how you were able to track the poaching ring to Ruacana?" Silas asked while he looked through the photos.

"Yes. The truck belongs to a man called Pik Malan."

"How did you find that out?" Silas asked.

"Jonathan Tuhadeli told us that he owned Sundowner Safaris. He was able to track the license plate after Matt showed him the pictures," Patrick said. "Jonathan is the mayor in Khorixas."

Patrick was sitting across the hospital room, on the other side of Silke's bed. Silke was sitting up with two pillows against her back. She turned her head towards Patrick, but winced and rested back against the pillows.

"Should I get the doctor?" Matt asked. Silke looked very tired and drawn. They had brought her to the hospital earlier that day after driving through the night from Ruacana.

"No. I'm alright. I've just got to remember to stay as still as possible," Silke said. "The doctor says I have a concussion and a fractured rib."

"Sorry to have to put you through this, but we have to move quickly if we are to stand any chance of getting the poachers," Silas said.

"It's alright," Silke answered with a weak smile. "I had heard there was a poaching ring in Ruacana. I should have been more careful after my interview with the police captain. He was acting suspiciously, but I convinced myself that he was just caught off guard by my line of questioning."

"The captain in Ruacana was the person who kidnapped you?" Silas asked. "Are you sure?"

"Yes. I don't remember much about what happened after, but I do remember he was the one who assaulted me when I got back to my bungalow. The rest seems like a bad nightmare. I couldn't see anything, and I kept getting hit. It was awful, terrifying."

"And the two of you found her at Sundowner Safaris when you arrived in Ruacana?" Silas asked.

"That's right," Matt said. "It was actually Patrick who found her when he did an initial scout of the ranch. She was tied up in a shed by their airstrip with a sack over her head."

"But you did not rescue her then?" Silas asked, giving Patrick a searching look.

"No. It was daylight when I first came across Silke.

I was by myself, as Matt had gone into Ruacana to see if he could find out anything in town. I thought it best to wait until dark when I had Matt's help to get her out and we could leave quickly in the Rover."

The detective looked at all three of them.

"Well, you have done the right thing in bringing this to us. With the rhino horns as evidence, we will be able to break up this poaching ring. That will be all for now, but I must ask that you stay in Swakopmund while the investigation is ongoing. We will have some more questions for you when we get back from Ruacana."

Matt stood up and shook Silas's hand as he was leaving. "Thank you, detective. We'll be here when you get back."

*   *   *

Silke felt the warm, soft light against her face and, without opening her eyes, shifted the position of her head and shoulders on the pillow.

"Good morning," said a calm voice she recognized. It took her a moment to place it.

Silke's eyes snapped open. "Karl! How did you get here?"

"When you were brought in, the hospital found out you were a journalist and contacted the *Namibian Star's* office in town. I came out here as soon as I heard." Pain and worry were written across his face. "I'm very sorry I sent you after the rhinos. I had no idea you'd be in this much danger."

Silke shook her head. "You and I both know I had to go, so don't blame yourself. I'm a bit banged up, but I'm here and I'm going to recover." She paused. "You know what happened?"

"You asked too many questions, and the local police captain knocked you unconscious and handed you over to the poachers."

"At the Sundowner Safaris ranch, right?"

"So I understand."

"I had heard the name from one of the locals earlier the night I was kidnapped. And then I was rescued by two men, Matt and Patrick."

"Do you know who they are?"

"I think they introduced themselves, but it's a bit hazy. I was pretty well out of it."

"I had a brief chat with your rescuers earlier this morning. I have also managed to do a bit of research on the internet, and the local police told our office here a few things. Matt is an American named Matthew Harkes. He is in Namibia, in Damaraland, taking an unofficial look at the rhino population. The other man is a Namibian, an Owambo, who has been helping him. Fortunately for you, they were on the trail of the same poachers as you were. If they hadn't found you, you would probably be dead by now."

Silke quickly shifted the conversation away from that touchy subject. "But why would an American be here looking at rhinos?"

"He's a curator from the National Zoo in Washington."

"That's interesting."

"Yes. Do you remember we were puzzled by why the crime scene photos from America had been sent to you? How we thought that whoever had sent them here might have been trying to influence someone in Namibia?"

"Yes."

"Well, don't you find it an interesting coincidence that

those photos arrived here in Namibia about the same time as Harkes?"

"Do you think the story might have been intended for Matt? But why?"

"I don't really know. Maybe it was to convince him to go looking for the poachers."

Silke was not convinced. "Maybe."

"Here's something else interesting. Harkes's main contact over here has been Jonathan Tuhadeli."

"Tuhadeli...that name rings a bell. I think Matt mentioned him. Who is he?"

"He's the mayor of Khorixas. We've got an ongoing investigation into some government tenders he's favored to win to develop a series of lodges in Damaraland. He's a character who has been involved in a number of land deals over the years."

"Is he corrupt?"

"That's hard to say. He's one of the SWAPO men we'd like to do a lifestyle audit on, but his finances are pretty murky, so it is taking some digging. Shit never seems to stick to the man."

"You would think a curator from a zoo in America would be more likely to be working with conservation groups. What's his connection to a man like Tuhadeli?"

"That's a good question. Hopefully, I'll be sitting down with Harkes again in the next couple of days and will be able to ask him."

"I'd like to be there when you meet with him," Silke said.

* * *

A day later, Matt found himself talking to Silas Kabali again, this time at the Swakopmund police station on Garrison Street. The window was open, and a cool breeze was blowing in off the Atlantic Ocean.

"I'm afraid that when we got there, the poachers were already gone," Silas said, leaning back in his chair. He had a self-satisfied look on his face. "But with the horns you gave us, the testimony of the reporter and the confession of the police captain we have arrested, there is little doubt about what was going on. That poaching ring is definitely out of business, and it will make for a big story in the news."

"You didn't find anything else?" Matt asked. "No other evidence of what they were doing?"

"No. They obviously left in a rush. The main house looked a mess, but there was nothing of value left behind," Silas continued. "And that hangar by the airstrip had been burned to the ground. When they found out that the reporter and the horns were gone, they must have known the game was up. So, they destroyed whatever evidence was left and got out of there."

"You...didn't find anything in the hangar?" Matt asked.

Silas looked at Matt sharply. "No. We searched it very carefully. There was nothing left but ash and debris."

They didn't find the body, Matt thought quickly.

"Were you expecting us to find something?" Silas asked.

"No," Matt lied. "It was just that we didn't have time to search it very thoroughly. I was hoping that they might have left some other evidence."

Silas nodded.

"What about Pik Malan?" Matt asked. "What are you going to do about him?"

Silas looked at him. "He has probably left the country

already. We will name him to the press and contact our colleagues in other countries, but I think he will have gone to ground. We will be lucky to find him now."

"I suppose you are right," Matt said. "It is too bad you didn't catch him. He is a dangerous man."

"Yes, you are right, but time is on our side. We will not forget about him, no matter how long he stays hidden," Silas said. "Now, is there anything else you would like to tell me about the poaching or your time in our country?"

Matt looked at the man's face and realized he didn't know anything about the man Matt had killed. *The body is gone, and there is nothing to tie the death of the man back to me,* he thought.

"No. Nothing I can think of," Matt said.

*   *   *

The morning mist hung over Swakopmund like a cool, wet blanket. *This is an odd town,* Matt thought. Here on the edge of the world's oldest desert, the Atlantic Ocean cooled the town to the point that he needed to put on a sweater to take a morning walk on the pebble beach. He was meeting Karl and Silke in the *Namibian Star's* Swakopmund offices later that morning. Two days earlier, the newspaper had run the story about the rhino-poaching ring being discovered. The Ruacana police captain was now in custody. He had admitted that he had been accepting bribes to turn a blind eye to the poaching ring, but had insisted that he had never been part of the ring itself. There was no sign of Pik Malan. The newspaper had run Malan's picture with the story and indicated that he was a suspect the police were looking for and wanted to question. The story contained only some basic background information on Malan. He was a farmer whose family had lived in Namibia since the early 1900s. The investigation, at least at this early stage, had found no link to the South African military. Malan was just a violent man looking to make money.

What's the connection to South Africa and the Maryland rhino? Is there one? Matt wondered.

Matt knelt down and picked up a pebble that had been smoothed by the constant action of the waves crashing over it. He took off his shoes and walked into the surf, letting the cold water crash up to his knees. He rubbed his fingers over the smooth surface of the stone and then threw it as far as he could into the Atlantic. The poaching ring was broken, but something was still missing, and it gnawed at him.

"Matt!" He heard a voice call out, just audible above the waves. He turned around. It was Patrick walking towards him. Matt waved at him and waited for him to arrive. Together, they walked further along the beach, the waves washing over their feet.

"What is the plan for today?" Patrick asked him.

"I have a meeting with Silke and Karl from the *Namibian Star* at ten this morning. You're welcome to join me for that if you like."

"No, I don't think I will," Patrick said. "I should be returning to Khorixas to give Tuhadeli his vehicle back, and he owes me some money."

"Will you continue working for him?"

"No, I think my time with him is over. I think maybe it is time I go home to Oshakati and make things right with my family. It has been too many years away, and if my mother and father are still alive, I should like to see them again, and to help them as they grow older. What about you? What will you do now?"

"I think I am ready to go home as well. There is a special woman there who I need to talk to," Matt said, thinking about Suzanne. The conversation with her while he'd been hunting deer in Maryland seemed like a lifetime ago, and he realized how much he missed their talks.

"That seems like a good idea. Do not take as long as I did to remember that home is a good place."

* * *

"Welcome, Mr. Harkes. Won't you take a seat?"

Karl ushered him into the office. Silke was seated in front of the small desk and made an effort to stand up and greet him.

"Please, no need to get up." Matt hurried across and shook the hand she offered to him.

"Thanks. It is still a bit painful to stand," Silke admitted, sitting back down in her chair. "Once I'm up, it's alright, but it is the getting up that is a chore."

"Can we get you anything?" Karl asked.

"No, thanks. I just had coffee with Patrick. He's taking the truck to get gas. He's looking to head back to Khorixas later today."

"I was hoping to thank him in person," Silke said, a look of disappointment crossing her face.

"I know he's very happy that you are safe, and I'll be sure to pass along your thanks to him before he leaves." That seemed to mollify Silke somewhat. Matt sat down next to Silke as Karl took his place behind the desk.

"Shall I get straight to the point?" Karl asked.

"That is always the best way to go." Matt smiled at him. "I suppose you want to know what Patrick and I were doing at Sundowner Safaris?"

"That's certainly part of it," Silke said. "And let me add, I am very grateful you showed up."

"Is this off the record?" Matt asked. "I don't mind talking to you, but I don't want to find myself plastered all over the morning newspaper just now."

Karl laughed. "Don't worry. We have a great story already. But we both believe there is something more complex going on with these rhinos, and we'd like to get your perspective on it. So, we will keep this off the record, but we may come back to you at a later time for an actual interview. Is that alright with you?"

"That sounds fair enough. What makes you think there is something more complex going on than a simple case of poaching?"

Matt listened as Karl and Silke told him the story about how they had received the crime scene photos from America and their concerns about why they had been sent to the *Namibian Star*.

"That is odd," Matt agreed. "I had assumed that the photos had been widely distributed when I read your story. I didn't realize that you were the only news outlet with them. So, you think you were being manipulated, but to what end?"

"We think the story might have been targeted to you," Karl answered. "So you would make a link between the death of the rhino in Maryland and the poaching here. You said when we first talked that you were here to do an informal assessment of the rhinos in Damaraland and that Jonathan Tuhadeli was your main contact here."

"Yes, that's right, not that he has been much use, though he did put me in touch with Patrick, so I shouldn't be too critical. You see, the death of the rhino in Maryland was very damaging to the prospects of keeping a sustainable population of captive black rhinos in zoos on a number of levels. The rhino was very valuable. As a freshly caught wild animal, it would represent a new bloodline in the captive population, so that was a huge loss. Perhaps more damaging is that it will now be far more difficult to import live rhinos from range countries. The slaughter of the rhino, particularly the circumstances of it, has the potential to shut down any imports for a long time to come."

"So, what were you assessing the rhinos for, and for whom? The National Zoo?" Silke asked.

"No. A partner company that is focused on frozen zoos."

"Frozen zoos?"

"Freezing genetic material from threatened species as a means of protecting their genetic diversity and thus their survival," Matt explained.

"Is that possible?" Silke asked.

"Yes, it has been done with a number of captive species already," Matt answered. "The theoretical part is collecting a complete cross section of genetic material from a wild population. That was partly what I came here to assess, to see if it would be possible to collect genetic material from the Damaraland black rhino population."

"And what did you conclude?" Karl asked.

"It is far too early to draw conclusions. It will be a real challenge, but the company is very committed to trying. It was involved in the export of the rhino that died in Maryland."

"Was it that company that put you in touch with Jonathan Tuhadeli?"

"Yes. Why so much interest in Tuhadeli?"

"Well, the name rang a bell when you first mentioned it," Karl answered. "Tuhadeli is a character we have been trying to find out more about. His main interest in Damaraland is a government tender on several high-end lodges that the government wants to build in the desert. He heads up a company called Ontstaan Properties that is looking to place a bid. But we have discovered that Tuhadeli's Namibian company has links to a South African company of the same name."

"What are you suggesting, that the American company that sent me here is investing in Tuhadeli's land deal?" Matt asked.

"No," Karl answered. "We haven't found any evidence of American involvement in the land deal. I can't see why an American conservation company would be involved in that anyway. We think the money behind the deal might come from China."

"China?" Matt said. "Why would China be investing here?"

"The Chinese have been investing in Namibia for almost three decades," Karl answered, "but there has been an increasing backlash against them and their companies among Namibians. Any tenders the Chinese bid on these days would get intense scrutiny, and the Chinese don't want that sort of publicity. So, they have been looking for a front company with deep African connections through which they can channel their money. We think Ontstaan Properties could be that front company."

Matt thought about that. "But why are the Chinese so interested in Damaraland?"

"Rhino horn," Karl answered. "There's not much else of value in Damaraland."

"That makes sense," Matt said. "Demand in China is one of the real engines driving the surge in poaching. When ground up into a powder, the horn is used as a cure for everything from headaches and minor pains to impotency."

"When I talked to Mphuswe Sithole, the director of Rhinos International," Silke interjected, "she told me that the traditional medicine markets in Asia are exploding— that was her word. She said that poached horns used to go to Yemen to be made into dagger handles, but now most of them go to Asia."

"Yes, that is true," Matt said. "The markets in Asia are really pushing a number of wildlife species to the brink of extinction—rhinos included. It is one of the reasons collecting genetic material from the Damaraland rhinos is so important."

"If the Chinese invest in Tuhadeli's resorts, it could give them unfettered access to the last free-roaming population of black rhinos in Africa," Karl said. "They would likely use that access to quietly cull animals for their horns."

"I just can't see the company that sent me here getting involved in all of that," Matt said. "They want to save rhinos, not kill them."

"Maybe that's the connection," Silke said. "Maybe they sent you here and introduced you to Tuhadeli in the hope that you might find out what Tuhadeli was up to."

"So they didn't want me to investigate just the poaching ring but Tuhadeli too?"

"Do you know any Afrikaans, Matt?" Silke asked. "Do you know what 'ontstaan' means?"

"No, I don't. You lost me there."

"It means 'inception,'" Karl said. "We are worried that the development of the lodges in Damaraland is just the beginning of something much larger."

Chapter 13

"How's the turkey, Matt?"

"It's really good, thank you."

Suzanne's mother Jeanette gave him a warm smile and offered him another portion. It was Christmas Day, and he was having dinner with Suzanne's family at her parents' Bethesda home in the suburbs of Washington, DC. It was a two-level stone building with an extensive and well-kept garden. Like many of the other houses in the neighborhood, it sported Christmas lights around the windows at the front of the house and in the trees next to the driveway.

Matt enjoyed the season and all its trappings, even though he didn't usually do much to celebrate it. In years past, he would have driven across the Bay Bridge to Maryland's Eastern Shore and spent the holidays with his parents, but both had now passed away. The holidays had always been a subdued affair with his parents: a small tree with everyone buying each other one small gift. Christmas dinner likewise had been a simple affair. The family had stayed away from the traditional turkey meal, instead usually eating venison steaks from one of his father's hunting trips. It had been a simple time of the year when they had celebrated family, and, in the years since his parents had died, he had missed it.

"Have some more," Jeanette said. "There really is plenty. We will be eating turkey sandwiches and soup until February if you don't."

"Thanks, but I am not sure I could eat another bite. And I think dessert is still to come." The meal Suzanne's parents had put on was a feast. The turkey itself was at least twenty pounds. When Matt had first seen it, he had thought there must be more people coming to dinner, but it was just him, Suzanne and her parents.

"It's all for you." Suzanne had laughed when she had seen his worried face.

Roast potatoes, greens, gravy, carrots, sweet potatoes and apple and cranberry sauce. The table had been laid with the family's best china and crystal, and the Christmas tree in the corner of the dining room sparkled with green, red and white lights.

"Dessert is still to come," Jeanette agreed, "but you can still have some more of the main course. We need to put some weight on you after your trip to Africa. You're looking tanned, but a bit thin. Are you sure you've been eating properly?"

"So, how was Africa?" Suzanne's father Bill asked. "Suzanne tells us you were over there for a couple of weeks."

"Yes. I just got back this past Monday. I went over to do a preliminary assessment of a rhino population in Namibia for a private company that is working with the National Zoo on collection sustainability," Matt said.

"On what? Sustainability? What do you mean by that?" Bill asked.

"Basically, due to the small size of certain populations of

animals in captivity, those populations need to be managed carefully to make sure they remain genetically viable in the future. Rhinos, black rhinos in particular, are a prime example of an animal population that needs extensive management if they are to thrive in the future. "

"I'm sure Matt doesn't want to bore us all with his zoo and safari stories," said Suzanne.

"That's okay," Matt said. "I'm always happy to talk about the animals or going on safari. It was the first time I have been to Namibia, and I must say it is a striking country."

Matt took a sip of his wine and warmed to the topic. It was pleasant to be with Suzanne and her parents again. He sometimes felt awkward in social settings, something he put down to his many years of bachelor life, but it was different when he visited Suzanne's family. It was as close to a feeling of home as he had had in a long time.

"Are you sure you don't want some more roast potatoes?" Jeanette offered.

"Mother, would you leave Matt in peace? He knows where the serving spoons are if he wants more," Suzanne chided.

"Oh, alright, but you do need to eat more, Matt. I worry about you sometimes."

Matt gave a short laugh. "I worry about me sometimes as well. I have to admit, there was a time while I was in Africa when I was a bit worried about my diet as well. I went several days when I had nothing but canned beef and beans." The memory of Patrick cooking the meals on the small camping stove next to the Rover brought a smile to Matt's face. "Actually, it wasn't too bad. Not too bad at all."

"That's awful!" Jeanette said. "I don't know how you

manage when you go on these trips into the field. Suzanne is always telling us what you are up to, you know. You should settle down at some point."

"Mother!" Suzanne said, flushing slightly and smiling at Matt.

"Did you see any animals while you were there?" Bill asked.

"Yes. You should have seen the desert elephant we found, or more like the elephant who found us. He came as close to me as you are, perhaps closer. My friend Patrick..." Matt took another sip of wine. Mentioning Patrick's name gave him pause. In the short time they had known each other, a friendship had developed. Perhaps it was a connection born of the shared danger as much as the long journey.

I wonder what Patrick is doing for Christmas, Matt thought. *I hope he has found his family again and made peace with them.*

"My friend Patrick couldn't believe it when the elephant appeared right behind the Rover," Matt continued. "I almost had to pull him back into the truck. For a moment, it was as if his feet were rooted to the ground. The elephant stayed with us a while at the water spring. It was a real highlight."

"Matt got some beautiful photos," Suzanne said. "He's quite the photographer."

"We'd love to see them. Perhaps the next time you come around you could bring them. But you said you were looking for rhinos. Did you see any?" Bill asked.

"No, Bill, I didn't. That was a disappointment, but not a real surprise given the short time I was over there. It is one of the challenges we will face if the project goes ahead. It is such a large, desolate area that the rhinos live in, you really have to know the land and the behaviors of the animals to stand a chance of finding them."

The conversation flowed as they had dessert and then moved to the living room for coffee. Matt was careful to leave out any part of the story that touched on poaching. That could only lead him to one place, and he didn't want to talk about it tonight, not with Suzanne, not with her parents, not on Christmas.

The thought kept coming back. *I killed a man. The man was going to rape Silke, and I killed him.*

The killing had been done in a moment of rage, but the cover-up had been calculated. He knew that if Patrick hadn't been there to pull him off, he would have delivered even more blows to the man's head. He remembered telling Patrick that he wasn't in Namibia to kill, but when the moment had arrived, he had killed without a moment's hesitation. After he had taken the man's pulse and realized he was dead, he had known that he would have to do something to cover their tracks. Silke was hurt, and the last thing they had needed was the men behind the poaching looking for them and the missing rhino horns.

Taping the man into the chair and setting him and the hangar ablaze had been meant to throw the poachers off the trail, at least for a short time. When the blaze had died down, he had known they would find the charred remains of a body with the chair. He had hoped they would think it was the body of the journalist. He had also doused the crates with plenty of fuel to hide the fact that he had taken the horns. Even if the poachers guessed that the horns were gone, he had hoped that their first inclination would have been to blame the man they had left guarding Silke.

Matt had meant to tell the police about killing the man

after they had raided the farm and found the body. But when the police had found no remains in the hangar, he had kept quiet. He regretted not speaking now, but in that moment, when he had been talking to the police, bringing up a dead man they didn't know about had seemed foolish.

Matt had thought about that on the flight home. The poachers must have found the remains of the man the morning after he had burned the hangar down. If they had thought it was Silke, they would have certainly gotten rid of the remains quickly. He'd put enough fuel on the body to make it unrecognizable after it had burned. They would not have realized their mistake until they saw the news story with her byline.

His time in Africa seemed surreal now. The trip had flown by. He had given Silke and Karl his contact information so they could reach him if they needed anything. Silke had told him she was going back to South Africa. Apparently, the *Herald* newspaper in Johannesburg had some interest in hiring her. She and Karl had promised to keep him up to date on anything they found out about Ontstaan Properties and Tuhadeli.

What is really going on in Namibia and South Africa? Matt wondered. *Why did Reddman choose Tuhadeli to be my contact there? And who sent the* Namibian Star *the Baltimore crime scene photos? This is about more than the Damaraland rhinos and collecting genetic materials to help keep the captive population viable.*

"Would you like another coffee?" Suzanne asked him, touching him lightly on his arm.

It was three days since he had gotten back from Africa, and he was still feeling jet-lagged. He tried to repress it but couldn't help a small yawn. "Sorry. I was just thinking about Africa. I think I'll need one."

Suzanne stood up and went to kitchen to join her mother.

Suzanne's father lit a fire that roared to life. "There's nothing like a good fire on Christmas night," he said. "It is one of my favorite traditions this time of year. Takes me back to my childhood when my dad would sit us all down after Christmas dinner and hand presents out around the fire. Ever since, I've always thought it a bit odd that people do the presents in the morning around the Christmas tree. I gave in to that tradition when I married Jeanette. Her family was all about presents in the morning, but I have hung on to a bit of my past with this fire. We have coffee in front of it every year after Christmas dinner."

"That sounds like a family tradition worth having," Matt agreed. "It seems like you blended the best from both your families into a wonderful Christmas of your own."

The two of them sat quietly looking at the fire for a few moments, each absorbed in his own thoughts.

"You know," Bill said, "Jeanette and I always thought that you and Suzanne should have gotten together."

Matt looked at Suzanne's father and leaned back on the couch. Bill was in his late sixties and had been retired for a few years. He'd been a researcher at the National Institute of Health just down Rockville Pike from the neighborhood he and Jeanette had lived in for most of his career. NIH had been where he had met Jeanette. They had crafted a comfortable life together, and retirement looked good on the couple. Matt had always liked them but had never talked about Suzanne with them. He didn't usually talk about his personal life with anyone, but something was different now, a subtle change had occurred, and he felt comfortable talking about Suzanne.

"We have been a bit star-crossed over the years, but the thought has occurred to me on more than one occasion as well," Matt admitted. "The timing has just always been off." Matt had accepted Suzanne's first marriage, as she was engaged when they had met. But her second marriage had always baffled him. *Why didn't she see what was right in front of her all these years?*

"I think that might be changing," Bill said and smiled. "I never really did see why she married Mike and Phil. Don't get me wrong. They were good men, but not right for Suzanne. For whatever reason, I think she felt a pressure to be married, a pressure to start a family, but I think the two divorces have made her move beyond that. She is in a better place now. What Jeanette and I want most for her now is to be happy."

The fire crackled, and Matt sat forward to better feel its warmth. He liked Bill and Jeanette. They had always been kind and welcoming to him over the years, but he had always been the other man in Suzanne's life. "I'd like to see that as well," Matt admitted.

"What are you two conspiring about in there?" Jeanette called from the kitchen.

"Just football," Bill lied. "Matt is trying to convince me that the Ravens are going to win another Super Bowl this year."

"I didn't realize you were a football fan," Suzanne said as she brought the coffee through. "Dad's got season tickets to the Redskins. You two should go to a game next year."

"I'm an ardent Ravens fan," Matt lied.

Suzanne sat down next to him on the couch, looked at him quizzically and handed him his cup. "Well, that is settled then. Dad can show you a schedule of the home games, and the pair of you can go to one."

They all sat in silence for a while, enjoying the fire, the coffee and each other's company. Suzanne sat close to Matt, letting her leg press easily against his. After the coffee was done, Bill and Jeanette excused themselves and went into the front room to watch some television. Suzanne leaned in more heavily and lifted Matt's arm so he could drape it around her shoulders. She then pressed closer, relaxing her head against his shoulder.

"This is nice," she said in a soft voice. "I am really glad you've come."

Matt took a deep breath and relaxed himself. "I am glad I came as well. Why has it taken us so long to get to this place?" The deep warmth of her body next to his felt good. It was as if a barrier that had been between them for years was falling away in a matter of minutes.

"Perhaps we both needed to follow our own paths for a while before we came together."

He leaned his face against her head. After a while, she turned her face towards his and kissed him softly on the lips. After a moment, she pulled back and stroked his cheek with her hand.

"Matthew Harkes, you taste like Christmas."

Chapter 14

The day before she flew to South Africa, the staff of the *Namibian Star* gave Silke a send-off braai at Karl's house, complete with barbecued chicken, boerwors and plenty of beer. She knew saying goodbye to the close friends and colleagues of the last seven years would last well into the night. These were the people she had worked with, argued with and stayed up late with, struggling to get stories right. At one point, early in the evening, she almost convinced herself that she wanted to stay in Namibia.

"It's hard to say goodbye, isn't it?" The question interrupted her thoughts as she sat quietly on the edge of the party thinking about her future. It was Paulus Sealola, the paper's circulation manager. Though their jobs had little to do with each other, at a small paper like the *Namibian Star*, everyone knew everyone. Paulus was a shy, polite man who went about his work with quiet efficiency. He sat down next to Silke.

"Yes, it is. More difficult than I had imagined it would be," she said. "Seeing everyone here together like this makes me wonder if I've made the right decision."

"You must go," Paulus said. "Everyone here is very proud of what you have done. For most of us here, the

Namibian Star is our home, Namibia is our home. When we talk to our friends now and tell them that we work at the *Namibian Star*, they ask us if we know the lady who writes about the rhinos, the lady who has made our paper famous around the world. The boys and I might spend the rest of our careers working in the streets of Windhoek, getting the newspaper out to the shops and to the people, but you can move on to one of the big papers in South Africa now, and that will make us even prouder. We will be able to say that we knew you when things were just starting."

Silke looked at Paulus a moment. "There's part of me that feels I've had enough of this rhino story, but it is what will get me my next job. Whatever paper I end up at, I am sure they will want me to follow up on what I have already written. I was very lucky to come away from this last story at all."

"Luck favors the talented," Paulus said. "I do not know everything that has happened, but the stories you write make people care. Even if luck has played a part, luck comes to those who work hard. You must take your talent and reach more people with it. Namibia is just the start of your own story. Do not be afraid to move on to the next chapter because you will be leaving some old friends who work at a small newspaper in a small country." He smiled at Silke, "You should join the others again. This braai is for you, after all."

"Such wisdom from the circulation manager of a small paper in a small country," Silke said. "I will miss you all very much, you know."

* * *

The next morning, Karl drove her to the airport. The drive passed in silence, and then they sat in the departure area for another half hour without speaking. Everything that needed to be said had already been said, and both of them knew it. Yet, when the time came for her to go, saying goodbye to Karl was surprisingly difficult. Both knew that an important chapter in both of their lives was coming to a close.

"You'll let me know that you've made it there alright?" Karl said when it was time for her to go through customs.

"Of course, I will."

He wrapped her in his arms in a big but gentle hug, and she buried her face into his neck and held him close. For a moment, she didn't want to let go of this man who had brought her to Namibia, this man who had helped launch her career, this man whom she loved. But she knew it was time. Then she stepped back from him and ran her hand down his arm, briefly holding his hand and squeezing it gently.

"Thanks for everything, Karl. I'll write you and let you know how things go with the *Herald*."

He smiled and nodded, but said nothing. She realized that this goodbye was difficult for him as well. She turned and walked towards customs and then into the waiting lounge for international flights. When she was through customs, she looked back, but Karl had already gone.

* * *

Sitting at her desk in the *Herald*'s Durban office, Silke rubbed the back of her neck. It still bothered her occasionally, and she had trouble turning her head when she first woke, but over the course of the day the stiffness and pain would fade away. She turned her head, stretching her neck as she rubbed it. Looking at property reports from the deeds registry was monotonous work. *So much for the glamor of investigative reporting,* she thought as she smiled to herself.

She had been at the *Herald* a couple of weeks. Her new boss, Marjorie Clemments, had been one of the editors Silke had interviewed with when she had come to Johannesburg after spending some time with her parents in Craddock. Marjorie was chief of the newspaper's Durban office, and the two had struck it off well. Once she had been hired, Silke had filled Marjorie in on the work she had been doing on the rhino story with the *Namibian Star*. Marjorie had agreed that there were some interesting possibilities with the story. The newspaper prided itself on exposing corruption in government and business, and the newspaper had been reporting on rhino poaching for years. Silke had been glad that Marjorie was taking an interest in the rhino story, as it wasn't a story she was ready to let go of yet.

Marjorie also had a keen sense of where and when a story needed more research. "You'll find more useful information doing some hard research than charging off into the bush," Marjorie had told her. "You helped bring down a poaching ring in Namibia, but if you are right and there's a deeper story here, you need to find out who is behind the trade. Find out where the money is coming from and where it is going, and you are likely to catch the bigger game. Find out who Ontstaan Properties is connected to and what deals Ontstaan is involved in. Find out if there are any patterns that might shed some light on what is happening to the rhinos in this part of the world."

Silke stretched again. She had been looking at property

reports for days now, and a pattern was starting to emerge. Whenever a large ranch was sold in South Africa, Ontstaan Properties usually served as the middleman, and the purchaser was often either an African National Congress official or someone closely tied to the ruling party. Silke had recorded the names of the ANC officials and the farms they had purchased on a spreadsheet: Mpho Dlamini, ANC Minister of Sports: Empangeni Safaris; Theophilus Moloi, Deputy President of the ANC Youth League: Mkuzi Game Ranch; Mthoe Tatane, Regional ANC Chairman in Kwa-Zulu Natal: Ocean Side Game Ranch; Phumalani Mbalulu, Treasurer of the ANC in Kwa-Zulu Natal: Pongola Private Game Ranch. The list went on.

The only one not on this list is the president, Silke thought. The new president of the country had won a contentious election the previous year, marking a remarkable comeback from his suspension from the ANC when he had been a firebrand president of the ANC Youth League. *That would really make this story.* She smiled to herself at the thought.

"How's the digging going?" Marjorie asked as she stuck her head through the door.

"Pretty well, I think. Some interesting names are popping up."

"They usually do when you start to dig a little," Marjorie said. "Why don't you take a quick break and fill me in on what you've found so far." Marjorie walked into Silke's office and sat down. "Let's hear it."

Silke took a deep breath and began. "First, Ontstaan Properties is a South African company that owns or controls vast sections of land in the least urban parts of South Africa. It specializes in high-end game ranches that cater to foreign tourists. Further, Ontstaan is connected to a company in Namibia by the same name, which seems to be compiling an equally impressive inventory of game farms in that country."

"Interesting," Marjorie said. "So, who owns Ontstaan?"

"That is one question I haven't been able to answer yet. The ownership is filtered through a series of numbered companies. The only principal I have been able to identify is a man called Jonathan Tuhadeli, a local Namibian politician who runs the Namibian branch of the operation. But I can certainly identify a lot of people who are involved with Ontstaan."

"Such as?"

"Well, the most interesting thing I've found so far are the names of the people who have bought farms through Ontstaan," Silke said. "Over the past few years, almost all the purchases of large game ranches in South Africa have been by prominent ANC officials or people who are closely connected to the ruling party. And the prices paid for these properties seem to have been well under market value when I compare them to other properties that are listed with other companies."

"That is interesting," Marjorie agreed. "Any other patterns showing themselves yet?"

"Yes. As I have found each property listing, I have gone to each ranch's website and checked to see what species they list as being present on the ranch. Elephant, giraffe, leopard, lion, cheetah and all sorts of antelope are listed on the sites. But only one species exists on all the ranches: white rhino. I've still got to do some more research and tabulating, but if the numbers keep on the same trajectory that they have been on so far, it wouldn't surprise me if Ontstaan Properties has brokered deals for properties that, when put together, have the largest privately held collection of white rhinos in the world."

"Really? But why would they have sold the properties if their interest is in controlling the captive white rhino population?"

"Ontstaan Properties doesn't only act as a real estate company. Ontstaan also offers its services as a ranch management company."

Marjorie thought for a moment. "So let's think this through. Ontstaan sells the properties to the politically powerful in the ANC at rates that are well below market price, and then Ontstaan continues to manage the properties in the name of these politicians? Is that your line of thought so far?"

"Yes. I think Ontstaan may be using ANC politicians to 'black wash' its operation, to give it an African face so the farms it runs won't be targets of the land redistribution program."

"That's an interesting theory," Marjorie said. "Is it just the names, the property prices and the rhinos that have you thinking along those lines?"

"At the moment, yes, and I realize that it is just a theory," Silke said. "What do you think?"

"Let me see the data you've been working on. I'd like to take a quick look at it."

Silke pulled the spreadsheet up on her computer and printed a copy. Marjorie took it from her, sat back and began to read. "You're right," Marjorie said after a while. "There are a lot of big ANC names on here, names of people that have very little involvement in game ranches and farming as far as I know. That certainly is a red flag, but not definitive evidence of any wrongdoing by anyone. Buying a farm cheap and being an absentee landlord is not a crime, and we'd have a hard time going after black African landowners, however corrupt they might be. Land redistribution is such a sensitive issue and has taken place so slowly that the newspaper would be hung out to dry by lawsuits and the government."

"So what do you think our next step should be?"

Marjorie looked at the spreadsheet again. "I think this is good as far as it goes, but if there is something going on, this list only hints at it. I've done enough stories like this to know that there is generally one thing that drives these people."

"Power?" Silke asked.

"That's part of it, but that is the end result. The more important factor is the money. Most of these ANC people are on government salaries. We need to find out what they are earning legitimately and how that compares with their lifestyles. They are also mostly elected officials in one manner or another, and elections these days are expensive things. We need to find out who has been donating what to whom. It's only by building a complete picture of what is going on that we will be able to find out the truth about this. How are these ANC people benefiting from these deals? My guess is that it is purely a matter of cash."

"That would seem like a fairly simple arrangement," Silke observed.

"It generally is. The whole ANC structure has been corrupted by money since they first took power in the 90s. It is a shame, but this goes on all around the world, big business buying its way into markets and using money as a means to access power and, through that, protection. In my experience, the crimes generally aren't all that sophisticated and clever, but they are insidious and undermine the rule of law over the long run. In this case, this 'black washing' would be a very simple but powerful tool. We will have to be careful about what we print, or it will be very easy for them to paint us as promoting a racist agenda, defending the entrenched interests of white farmers."

They both sat quietly for a moment. Marjorie, still looking at the spreadsheet, was the first to speak. "What would be helpful is if we had a source at Ontstaan. But we'd have to be careful, as we wouldn't want to tip our hand that we are doing an investigative story on the company. Do you have any ideas about who might be able to help?"

"As I said, the only person I know who is directly connected to Ontstaan is Jonathan Tuhadeli, but he is too deeply involved, and I don't think he is going to help us. The *Namibian Star* has been trying to investigate his property transactions for years." Silke paused. "There is also a family that has had some business dealings with Ontstaan, primarily through selling some property to Ontstaan, the Bezuidenhouts. They have been well established in Kwa-Zulu Natal since prior to the Boer War and have deep roots in the economic and political fabric of the province."

"No need to tell me about the Bezuidenhouts. They are about as well connected a family as there is in this part of South Africa. Anyone else?"

"Well, there is one possibility, but it is a bit of a long shot."

Chapter 15

Cecile Reddman walked across the garden towards the main house. It was early February, and she had returned home to her family's game ranch in Kwa-Zulu Natal. Her father still lived in the house, though he was well into his eighties now. Although he had given up the running of the farm, he stayed active, maintaining a beautiful garden. As she walked past the flowerbeds at the base of the small hill that ran gently up to the house, memories of her childhood came back to her.

She had been a tomboy when she was younger, playing rugby and football with her brother on the lawn that spread out around the house. They both had had the run of the ranch and had often spent all day in the bush with the children of the hired help. She smiled as she walked up the hill towards the house. The sun was shining, the garden bursting in color, and it was good to be back home, good to be back in Africa.

"Meme C," a familiar voice called out from behind her.

Cecile turned and saw Boysen coming up the hill behind her. Boysen was the gardener and was locked in an ongoing battle with her father about the flowerbeds. He was perhaps ten years younger than her father and equally lively.

"Meme C, it is good to see you home again," Boysen said and held out his hand. Cecile took his hand and shook it gently.

"It is good to see you as well, Boysen. The garden is looking beautiful this year. You must be keeping my father busy."

"Dr. Samuel does not listen to anything I tell him," Boysen said and sighed. "I have been a gardener my whole life, and he still tries to tell me where to plant things. You must tell him that I know what I am doing."

Boysen was from Mozambique. He had left the country decades before, fleeing the violence as the nation was torn apart in the fighting for independence. He had come to South Africa for work and peace. He had arrived at the ranch over thirty years ago. From his first day on the farm, he had called Cecile's father Dr. Samuel. Her father had never attended medical school, but the title had stuck. Now, most of the farm workers referred to her father as Doctor, much to his amusement.

Cecile laughed. Boysen and her father had been battling about the flowerbeds for almost twenty years. "You know my father listens to me even less than he does to you," Cecile said. "You must convince him yourself, hey."

The trip had been tiring for Cecile. She and Steven had flown in from California but, instead of stopping in South Africa, had traveled on to Namibia for a few days, where Steven had had some business to take care of. Despite growing up in South Africa, Cecile had never traveled to Namibia before. Her brother Jannie had fought there when he had done his national service with the South African Defense Force. Most young South African men of the day had dreaded being called up to fight in the bush war that had raged for years, but not Jannie. He had volunteered to go as soon as he was old enough. Born and bred in the South African bush, he was a soldier at heart.

Jannie had come home with stories about a hot and harsh land, about the battles he had fought in and the men he had killed. Cecile had been intrigued and horrified at the same time. She had lived a protected life on the ranch and then, when she was old enough, at a private boarding school in Durban. Her brother's stories had opened a wider world to her. The thought that her brother had killed men had shocked her at first. But as she looked back on it now, she wondered why she had been surprised. She loved him, but she knew that he was a hard, even dangerous man.

She also knew that those qualities were what initially had attracted her to Steven. He was a reflection of her brother in many ways. He was charismatic and exuded a confidence and power that she had found deeply alluring. When she was younger, that had been immensely attractive. But now, as the years passed, she found herself drifting away from Steven. There were moments when he could still surprise her and the old attraction would rise again, but those moments were increasingly rare. He was a cold man, and she now craved warmth. He was ambitious and driven, and she wanted to be settled and content. She was growing tired of her life with Steven. She wanted something different, something that would fill the grow-ing void in her life.

"Boysen!" a voice shouted from the top of the hill. "What stories are you telling my daughter now?"

Boysen looked up the hill, shook his head and then looked back at Cecile. "Dr. Samuel is a very difficult man to work for." He smiled. "He will ask me about watering the flowerbeds at the back of the house, but he has been using the hose all morning. He is impossible."

"You and my father have been working on this garden together for twenty years. I would have thought you would have had this all sorted out by now." Boysen and her father had been enjoying their good-natured sparring for years. Cecile often thought it was what kept them both going.

"Boysen, you need to water the flowers at the back of the house, you know. They will die of thirst by the time you get around to it," Samuel growled. "If you're not careful, I will get a younger gardener who can do things twice as fast as you can."

Boysen gave Cecile a knowing look.

"Why are you walking?" Samuel asked Cecile. "I saw the car pull up, but you weren't in it. I thought for a moment that you must have missed your flight and didn't arrive at the airport."

"I just had Leonard drop me off about a mile back. It's been a long journey, and I wanted to stretch my legs and get a bit of fresh air. Anyway, I love walking through the garden at this time of year."

Near the top of the gentle incline was a flowerbed with an array of purple flowers. As Cecile and Boysen came up to it, her father reached down and picked one of the flowers.

"A kleinbosviootjie for you, my dear," Samuel said as he handed her the flower. "This was always your favorite color as a child." He had planted a bed of the bush violets every year since Cecile had moved to America. He tended the bed of flowers himself. Each time she returned home, he would have a vase of them waiting for her in her room.

Cecile took the flower and put it to her nose. It smelled

of Africa. "You always were such a charmer, father. It's no wonder mother stayed with you all those years."

"Your mother was a wonderful woman, but I think it was you and Jannie that she stayed for more than me. She never did develop much of a taste for life on the ranch."

"You do mother a disservice, father. She was very happy here with you. It was the life she chose."

"Perhaps," Samuel agreed. "But she did love her trips into Durban on a regular basis, just like you do."

Samuel was right. Like her mother, Cecile loved the city with all its refinements. She had been a tomboy when she was a young girl, but life in boarding school had changed that. She had come out with a taste for luxury and the good life. In spite of that, she still cherished each time she could come back to the ranch. It had its rustic charms, and over the years her parents had invested in making the ranch a hunting lodge for high-end tourists.

"I really could use a cup of tea," Cecile said, "but first I must grab a hot shower and freshen up."

"Your room is ready, and I will have a tray of tea waiting for you when you are settled."

As they approached the house, a mud-covered pickup truck pulled up the driveway. A tall man in a brown shirt and a wide-brimmed hat got out and approached them. He was deeply tanned, and it was obvious he spent most of his time outdoors. He gave Cecile a cursory look and addressed her father.

"I'm here to see Jannie about a job. Is he about?"

Samuel looked the man over for a moment before he spoke. "This is about the game manager position, is it? What did you say your name was? It may seem old-fashioned to you, but on this ranch it is customary to introduce yourself before you start asking questions."

Cecile repressed a smile as she looked at the man and saw the muscles around his jaw tighten at her father's rebuke. He didn't like being talked down to, she decided. The tension was only apparent for an instant; then his face relaxed, and he smiled at Samuel.

"Apologies, meneer. My name is Pieter Malloy, and I am here to talk to Jannie about the game manager position."

* * *

Steven Reddman was in Oliver Tambo International Airport in Johannesburg. He had ordered a papaya juice and was sitting in the viewing area overlooking the tarmac. A row of three Airbus A340s sat outside the large circular window. He would be boarding one of them, South African Airways flight 207 from Johannesburg to Washington, DC. There would be a quick turnaround this time. He was heading to the States but would be back in Africa again in a couple of weeks. His plane sat next to a British Airways plane that had just arrived from London and was disgorging its passengers into the newly renovated airport. Despite all the hours he spent traveling around the world, he disliked flying.

He glanced at his watch. *Cecile will be home by now,* he thought. Reddman lifted his glass of juice and took a brief sip. He never drank alcohol while he was traveling. The airport was crowded with people rushing to catch connections or, like him, trying to get comfortable while they waited for flights later in the day.

His cell phone chirped. He picked it up and checked the display. It was Jannie, Cecile's brother.

"Hey, Jannie."

"Hey, Steven. How are you doing, man? Still waiting for your flight?"

"Yes, sitting here thinking. Not much else to do. Has Cecile arrived safely?"

"Yes, a couple of hours ago."

Reddman waited. Jannie wasn't a man who would call to make idle conversation. After a few moments, Jannie went on. "Steven, I want your input on a new hire I'm thinking of making."

Reddman frowned. "You don't usually ask me about hires in South Africa."

"Ja, but this one is from Namibia. With your contacts there, I thought you might be interested."

"What's his name?" Reddman asked.

"He told my father his name was Pieter Malloy."

"But?"

"It's Pik Malan."

Pik Malan. Reddman thought about this. Tuhadeli had provided him with back copies of the *Namibian Star* and all the stories that had run on the Ruacana incident and the poaching ring. He had also spent some time with Matt Harkes at the National Zoo in January. Reddman knew Pik Malan was a man on the run, wanted in his homeland of Namibia. Now, he was apparently looking for a job in South Africa.

"That is interesting. Did you think about calling the police?" Reddman asked.

"Ja, of course," Jannie answered. "But then I realized he

might be more useful in our hands. As you know, he has a lot of information about what's going on in Namibia, and I thought he might be more willing to pass that information on to us than to the police."

"Good decision not to call the police. You asked him about what happened in Ruacana?"

"Ja. He said he wants to lie low for a while and wondered if we could put him up at one of our bush camps. I said we might but in exchange he would have to tell us what was going on in Namibia. He thought about that for a bit and then agreed. To show he meant it, he told me an interesting story about getting rid of a body."

Reddman looked around the lounge to make sure no one was within earshot. "A body?"

"Ja. The guy is tough as nails, I tell you, but there is something that is not too bright about him. Apparently, he was off poaching rhinos in Damaraland and Etosha, and he knew nothing about the kidnapping until his boys called him and told him about it. It was the local police who panicked when the journalist started asking questions. The police grabbed her and then dumped her on Malan. That's where it gets interesting. When he gets back from his poaching trip, he finds his hangar burned to the ground and the charred remains of a body in the metal frame of a chair. He thinks one of his men has killed the journalist and done a runner with the rhino horn he had stored in the hangar. So, he gets rid of the body deep in the bush. He realizes that with a dead journalist, there is going to be a lot of heat in the area. He has a plane flying in later that day to pick up the rhino horns he has poached. When it arrives, he gets on and flies out of the country. It's only later that he realizes that the journalist is still alive. But by then it's too late, as the police are all over his operations back in Namibia."

Reddman ran his hand over his chin. Neither the news stories nor Matt Harkes had said anything about a body. "This does raise some interesting questions, doesn't it?"

"What do you mean?" Jannie asked.

"Well, with the journalist still alive and writing, whose body was in the hangar? And more interestingly, who did the killing?"

"I don't know. And I don't think Malan does either."

"Well, look. This guy could be helpful to us in the long run, but make sure he stays well hidden. No trips into town or any shit like that for him, okay? Best put him in one of the bush camps out in Maputaland for the time being while we think this whole thing through."

"Yeah, you got it. He doesn't seem like the type who will want to go into town anyway."

Reddman hung up and put the phone back into his pocket. If Pik Malan was to be believed, the charred remains of a body were buried deep in the bush somewhere in northern Namibia. *Could Matthew Harkes have killed a man?* he wondered.

Chapter 16

Back in Africa again, Matt thought. He reclined in the deck chair and took a sip of orange juice. It was still morning, but the heat and humidity were starting to grow. This was more like the Mid-Atlantic summers he was accustomed to in Maryland than the intense dry heat he had experienced two months before in Namibia.

"Have you ever had an opportunity to hunt in Africa?" Reddman had asked him when they had met in Washington in January. "My wife's family owns a game farm in South Africa. We'll be there in a few weeks. How would you like to join us?"

Natalie Harmon hadn't been surprised when he had brought up the possibility of flying to South Africa as a guest of Steven Reddman and his wife Cecile. Matt suspected Reddman had talked to her prior to inviting him on the hunting trip. He smiled at the thought of Natalie. She'd been a good friend over the years. He knew she was still in negotiations with Reddman about leasing the zoo's Conservation Biology Institute in Front Royal, and he had little doubt that was behind her endorsement of him going.

Matt was less sure about what he thought of Reddman

after the Namibian trip. The man had been pleased with Matt's initial assessment of Damaraland. However, Matt's assessment of the area and its rhinos would need to be followed up with a far more thorough and professional effort if there were to be any real prospect of collecting genetic material from the Damaraland rhinos. Thinking back on it, the whole Damaraland trip seemed poorly thought through. It was true that a poaching ring had been exposed and destroyed, but that hadn't been the goal of the trip, at least as it had been explained to him.

Reddman was an intimidating man and not someone easy to question, but Matt had not backed down. "What was the real reason you sent me to Namibia?" he had asked in January. "Was it really to investigate collecting genetic material from rhinos? Or were you hoping I would investigate the poaching ring or maybe even Jonathan Tuhadeli's land deals?"

Reddman had smiled. "It was really to investigate collecting genetic material from rhinos." He had grown serious. "Don't get me wrong. I am very glad you were able to help bring down that poaching ring. And I would greatly appreciate you telling me anything you might have discovered about what Jonathan Tuhadeli is up to. He is a man who needs watching. The more I know about the real situation in Africa the better. It's all connected. If we are to successfully collect genetic material from rhinos in Namibia, we are going to have to stop the poaching, and we are going to need the cooperation of politicians and businessmen like Tuhadeli, not just cooperation from conservation groups. They're the ones with the real power. But I have not been lying to you. I really asked you to go to Namibia to investigate collecting genetic material from rhinos."

And that was why Matt was now back in Africa. That and a lot of unanswered questions.

"How's the juice?"

Matt was suddenly jerked back to the present. He turned around in his chair. It was Cecile, Steven Reddman's wife. Matt guessed she was in her mid fifties, but she looked ten years younger. Tall, blonde and tanned, she was one of those people who held onto their beauty through the years. She had been quiet the previous night, but Matt was happy to see her.

"It's great, thanks. You really do have a beautiful property here."

"Thank you." Cecile smiled. "It's the old family house. It was built before the Boer War. It's been renovated several times since, but we've tried to keep some of the original history and feel to it. Steven wanted to apologize for not being here today. He had some urgent business to attend to on another ranch in Limpopo and left early with my brother Jannie to deal with it. But, if you don't mind, I'd be happy to take you out on an initial scout of the ranch to see if we can come up with a worthwhile trophy for you."

"That would be great," Matt said.

"Any thoughts on what you might like to take while you are here?"

"A kudu buck would be nice," Matt said. "I meant to do some hunting in Namibia when I was there a couple of months ago, but that didn't work out. If not a kudu, perhaps a nyala."

"I think we should be able to manage one or the other while you're here, perhaps both. Natal is well known for producing some spectacular kudu trophies. They can be incredibly shy animals—you see them and think you might have a clean shot, and then in a few steps they slip away, vanishing into the bush. Beautiful animals, though, and what is a good hunt if there is no challenge to it?"

"So you hunt as well?" Matt asked, genuinely interested. He didn't know many women who liked to hunt.

"Yes, I do, but I haven't in a while. Hunting is usually the purview of my brother Jannie, but I do enjoy getting out into the bush on occasion. It reminds me of my childhood here on the farm."

"Did you and your brother hunt a lot when you were younger?"

"More Jannie than I," Cecile said, "but we would run wild in the bush for what seemed like days on end. Every so often, my father would decide that we needed to learn some skills if we were going to be acting like wild animals, so he taught us both how to shoot and hunt. My brother took to it more than I did, but I enjoyed spending the time with my father doing something he loved."

Matt smiled at the memory of his own father and the hunting they used to do on Maryland's Eastern Shore. "That's how I got into hunting as well. I used to go duck hunting with my dad and our dog, General, near the Chesapeake Bay. Those were good times."

She gave Matt a wistful smile. "I've heard some good things about the Bay, but I must say I have never spent any time there. Surprising really, as I've been to Washington, DC, a number of times with Steven."

Matt found himself enjoying Cecile's company. He hadn't expected to find someone as genuine and friendly on this trip. He looked at his hostess and wondered how much she knew about rhinos, Genesis and her husband's business ventures.

"Why don't you get ready and we will head out into the bush," Cecile said.

"Sounds like a plan," Matt agreed, standing up with his glass in his hand.

"I'll take that," Cecile said and reached for the glass. She let her finger brush slowly against Matt's hand and smiled as she looked him in the eye. "I think you will find that hunting here is a challenge, but if done with some skill, the trophies can be spectacular."

Matt flushed a little. "I'd better get my rifle then," he said, returning her warm smile.

*   *   *

As she placed the glass on the kitchen counter, Cecile tried to decipher what she had read in Matt's gaze. Those blue eyes of his had caught her attention as soon as he had arrived at the ranch the previous afternoon.

Her attraction to Matt had been instant. When Steven had told her he was inviting Matt to the ranch for a two-week visit, she hadn't been thrilled at the idea. She had wanted a break from the endless social events that she and Steven either hosted or attended. Steven thrived on the events, even more so lately than usual. He had always been driven, but now he was becoming increasingly obsessed with Genesis Inc. To Cecile, the last year seemed like an endless stream of guests: politicians, zoo executives, scientists, businessmen, bankers and government bureaucrats. Most of the meetings were relatively painless, but the endless routine of business and socializing was draining. She'd hoped her trip to Africa would provide a break from all that, and then, at the last moment, Steven had told her Matt was coming.

"Who is he?" she had asked.

"Curator of large mammals at the National Zoo in Washington, DC. He went to Namibia and did some good work for me there. I'm thinking about recruiting him to Genesis."

"Do you really have to bring him all the way to our ranch in South Africa to do that?"

The hosting of Steven's business friends and contacts was tiresome enough in San Diego. The thought of one of Steven's middle-aged zoo contacts at the ranch for two weeks talking endlessly about good science and whatever animal he happened to specialize in wasn't appealing. She wanted to spend her time with her father, watching him and Boysen have their daily arguments about the flower-beds. She wanted to drive out onto the ranch by herself and visit favorite places from years past, landmarks that held a special place in her heart. She wanted to spend time with the wild animals. But mostly she wanted to be away from anything to do with Steven's professional life. She was being suffocated by the never-ending cycle of social-izing and business meetings. She wanted to break away and enjoy her Africa as she remembered it from when she was a child.

Then Matt Harkes had walked through the front door. He was tall and lean, and his blue eyes were kind and intelligent. She'd thought of little else since. Dinner had been a casual affair with just Matt, Steven, Jannie and her father. There weren't any other guests at the ranch that week, though a large party was scheduled to visit the fol-lowing weekend. Samuel had barbecued springbok steaks on the grill next to the pool at the back of the house. Matt had an easygoing way about him, and he had soon been conversing freely with her father, which was not always an easy thing. He had talked about good science and the animals under his care, and she had found herself listening with real interest.

"So what did you think of Namibia?" Samuel had asked Matt.

"A beautiful country if you like wide open spaces and blistering heat," Matt had said. "With some very interesting people as well."

"You have the bit about blistering heat right at least," Jannie had interjected. "South West Africa was a nest of vipers when I was there."

"Don't mind Jannie," her father had said. "His opinion of Namibia has been overly colored by the Border War. He won't even call the country by its new name even after all these years have passed."

"SWAPO terrorists all of them," Jannie had said, taking a swig from his beer bottle. "The only reason they have good roads now is because we built them. Mark my words, before too long, they will be like the rest of Africa."

"You fought in Namibia, I take it?" Matt had asked.

"Ja, with 32 Battalion, the Buffalos. We were based in northern Namibia, but most of the fighting was in southern Angola. We were the best soldiers in Africa at the time. The Battalion never should have been disbanded. It was a disgrace after what we did for the country."

"Matt didn't come all this way to talk about regional politics and hear your old war stories," Steven had said. "As interesting as they are, Jannie, I suspect he would rather hear about the ranches we are going to visit."

Cecile had watched the whole exchange with interest. A look of surprise had flashed across Matt's face during the conversation. Something Jannie had said had caught his attention. The conversation had drifted away from the war, and Cecile had found her gaze repeatedly being drawn to Matt's face. With some effort, she had remained polite, yet detached throughout the evening, worried that Steven would notice her attraction to Matt. It was a skill she'd honed over the years, hiding her inner feelings from those around her.

She needn't have worried. Steven had been far too focused on talking to Matt about Genesis Inc. and its role with both black and white rhinos in southern Africa to notice how drawn she was to their guest. She had listened quietly to their conversation while sipping a glass of white wine. The more she had listened to her husband, the more she had realized that she was growing tired of the man. Matt, however, was a breath of fresh air. She had tried not to stare, but at one point she had caught her father giving her a knowing but worried look as she had listened to something Matt was saying.

My attraction to Matt is obvious, she had thought. *But only to the man who really loves me. Steven wouldn't notice if I sat on Matt's lap.*

"What I thought we'd do is get you settled in and spend a day or two here hunting," Reddman had suggested to Matt. "Then we could head out past Hluhluwe-Umfolozi Game Reserve to a couple of other ranches further up the coast and spend some time out in the bush. How does that strike you?"

"That seems like a great idea," Matt had replied. "I can hardly wait to get out there. It seems like ages since I was able to enjoy a hunt."

"Excellent," Reddman had said. "And there's somebody I'd like you to meet, one of our new game managers. Jannie set him up at a bush camp out in Maputaland a few weeks ago. It is a bit of a drive, but I think you'll find him an interesting character." Reddman had smiled as he had said it. "We had an interesting chat with him the other day."

"I look forward to it. I always enjoy talking hunting with people who know what they are doing."

That's odd, Cecile had thought. *What's Steven up to? Why does he want Matt to meet the new game manager? Jannie's just hired the man, and he doesn't know the ranches, let alone the game on them.*

* * *

Now, as she stood there looking at Matt's empty glass, Cecile wondered what he was thinking. Matt's eyes had still been friendly, but there had been something else there as well. Surprise, perhaps. She had just made a pass at him, so he was entitled to that. He had also been assessing her, she realized. He was entitled to that as well. She was confident that he liked what he saw. She was very comfortable with her own beauty and how men reacted to it. Over the years, she had honed her skill in using it to get what she wanted. She knew she could manipulate men by simply flirting with them. It was a tool she had often used when she and Steven were at fundraising events. Countless times she had helped seal deals with subtle manipulation of men's emotions.

But this time it was different. She wasn't doing this to help Steven. She was doing this for herself. For the first time in many years, she desperately wanted to be with another man.

Matt's deep blue eyes had held her gaze for an instant. Cecile realized that he was equally skilled at masking his thoughts. Those blue eyes, with their kindness and deep intelligence, had been, for the moment, unreadable.

Just don't let there be rejection, she thought.

Chapter 17

Pik Malan leaned against the door frame of the small brick bungalow. His loaded hunting rifle was propped against the wall. The small, round building offered few comforts beyond a bed and a roof. There was a tap outside where he could get water to cook and wash with, but no sink, and there was a small fire pit within a circle of partially charred rocks that supported a metal grill. A stack of firewood stood around the back of the bungalow. It was all that he needed.

Jannie Bezuindenhout had driven him out to the camp several days earlier. It was deep in the bush at a game ranch in Maputaland not far from the Mozambique border. A small village clung to the side of a rocky hill four miles away. More a collection of little, thatched-roofed huts than a village, it gave the only hint that people lived in the area at all. No road led to it, just a foot trail that had been trodden down over the years.

This will be perfect, he thought. He preferred the solitude, but, more importantly, it was something he needed. Since he had fled Namibia, one step ahead of the police, he had traveled to various southern African countries, staying briefly with contacts before moving again. He didn't trust any of them. He knew, if it had served their interest, they would have handed him over to the authorities. If their situations had been reversed, Malan doubted he would have been as accommodating as they had been.

He knew they had been helping him out of fear. Fear was what he traded in, fear and illegal goods. It was all he knew. He'd been born on a small farm outside Tsumeb, a mining town southeast of Etosha in Namibia. His father, an alcoholic, had regularly beaten the farm workers. Pik had hated the man, but he had acquired the habit of violence from him. Pik had always been big and strong, and few people had been willing to stand up to him. He had gotten his first taste of poaching when he had come across two local Hereros hunting gemsbok on his father's farm. He had set about beating the pair, but they had offered to split the money that they would make selling the meat in town. He'd been young then, but he had soon found himself leading a network of local poachers in a bushmeat ring that had hunted farms between Tsumeb and Otjiwarongo. He hadn't looked back since.

He didn't trust Jannie, but he needed a place to lie low, and Jannie offered the best opportunity to do that. Malan had had a tidy operation running in northern Nambia and southern Angola, with the price of poached rhino horn so high. And rhino horn had been only part of his operation. Drug mules from Nigeria had routinely come down through Angola to drop off packages in Ruacana. He had taken the product and delivered it to contacts in Windhoek and Swakopmund who would prepare it for retail sale. He had been a middleman in the drug trade, and it had been a profitable business.

But everything had changed when the policeman had abducted the woman reporter.

Stupid fucking kaffir, Malan thought. *All the man had to do was to keep his head in a simple interview, and the reporter would have found nothing. And why the hell did they leave Edward of all people with her? Just being lazy bastards is what it was. Edward was the least reliable of all of them, and they left him in charge when that policeman dumped the reporter at the farm. One night of stupidity, and everything came down. All those fucking years of building the business wasted.*

The anger welled up in him again as he replayed in his mind that morning when he had returned to Sundowner Safaris from his last rhino-poaching trip.

* * *

When he pulled into Sundowner, he could see a small column of smoke rising above the bush in the direction of the runway. He immediately knew something was wrong. The drive back from Etosha had taken several hours. He had told them to just sit tight until he got there and he would take care of everything. The hangar had collapsed in on itself and was still smoldering when he drove up.

"Shit, Pik, Edward has gone and killed the reporter," one of his men told him as he got out of the truck. "We think he's taken the rhino horns, but it's hard to say for sure with the hangar torched. The reporter's body is still there in the remains of the chair, with a few bits of duct tape still attached. What do you want us to do?"

"You left Edward with the reporter and the rhino horns by himself? What the hell were you thinking?" Malan lashed out with his fist, catching the man squarely between the eyes. The man collapsed, blood spurting out as he covered his shattered nose. Malan kicked out with his boot as the man hit the ground, catching him in his stomach and knocking the wind out of him. The man lay on the ground gasping for breath as blood continued to pour from his nose.

"Nobody knows she was here, Pik. It will still be alright," another man said.

Malan rounded on him to hit him, but caught himself. He'd made his point with the other man, and he might need them again in the days to come.

"Listen, you stupid, kaffir-loving fucks. She was a reporter for the God-dammed *Namibian Star*. Do you know what reporters do? Do you know what they do?" Malan yelled at the man. "She was here looking into rhino poaching. There's only one damn group here poaching rhinos, and in case you haven't figured it out, that's us. She won't have just spoken to our stupid policeman friend. She'll have talked to any number of people in town. When she doesn't contact her office, there will be a lot of people up here asking a lot of questions that will lead them straight here."

The man looked at the ground and backed away as Malan yelled at him. "Sorry, Pik. We made a mess of this."

"That's an understatement. We've probably got a day, two at the most, to wrap up the operation here and get rid of any evidence. First thing, we need to get rid of the body. Put it in the back of my truck now. I'll take care of that myself."

He didn't want any of the men knowing where he buried the body. No body, no evidence of a murder.

"The rest of you, get the drugs and anything else packed away in your trucks, and head out to make any deliveries you can," Malan continued. "Nothing stays at the farm, got it?"

"What do we do after we've made the runs?" one of them asked "And what do we do about Edward?"

Malan thought for a moment, his rage starting to subside. The man he had knocked down had caught his breath and was standing up again, though blood was still running down his face. He moved away from Malan and joined the others.

"We're going to have to lie low for a while," Malan said. "Use the vehicles for the deliveries, but then get rid of them. Don't keep anything that will tie you back to Sundowner. Each of you will need to vanish for a while—whether it's here in Namibia, in South Africa or somewhere else, I don't give a shit. We just need to vanish. Edward will get his when the time comes, and that policeman as well if I ever see him again. Nobody screws me over like this."

Later that day, after burying the remains in a remote area of the ranch, Malan got on the plane that had been scheduled to pick up the shipment of rhino horns and left Namibia. He'd collected all the money from the house. He'd be losing out on the cash from the drug deliveries that his men would be making, but he didn't want to risk being caught in the country. He had plenty of cash stashed in banks around southern Africa, money he had saved for just such an eventuality.

* * *

A hornbill flew by the bungalow and landed on a nearby branch. It tilted its head sideways and looked at Malan as he leaned against the bungalow wall.

Shit, he thought. *I should have looked more closely at the corpse. I should have seen that it was Edward and not the*

168

reporter. How did he get himself strapped to the chair? The reporter must have had help.

He'd been playing the whole sequence of events over and over in his mind for weeks. He was already in Zambia when the news had broken about a rhino-poaching ring being smashed in northern Namibia. The local TV anchor had talked about a woman reporter for the *Namibian Star* who had been kidnapped by the gang but had escaped to tell the police. The broadcast had included a video of the rhino horns with a group of local police kneeling behind them as if they were trophies. *Those are my damn horns*, he had thought at the time. He had known he would have to keep a low profile. He had known that the police captain in Ruacana would be arrested, if he hadn't been already, and Malan had also been sure that he would be talking. It was not that the policeman had known much about the operation, but he had been paid regularly to look the other way, and he had been aware of both the drug trade and the trade in poached rhino horn.

Malan had been staying with one of his smuggling contacts in the Sunningdale suburb of Lusaka in Zambia, but the man had grown increasingly nervous. Malan had made the man plenty of money over the years, but he had known that would only count for so much.

"There is too much of this in the news. You can't stay here for long or they will find you," the man had said. "What if they catch one of your men? He will tell them you might be here. You've already stayed here too long."

Malan had known the man was right. He had needed to put more distance between himself and the Ruacana operation. The men he had worked with were reliable up to a point, but he had known he couldn't trust them not to get caught. He had told them to dump the vehicles after they had delivered the final shipment of drugs, but he wouldn't have been surprised if they had kept them. If the police caught them, he had known they would do whatever they needed to do to save their own skins, including selling him out.

Two days later, he had left Zambia. He had told the man he was going to Zimbabwe, and he had then left for Botswana. He had later been in Mozambique briefly and Zimbabwe, but he had never dared to stay in any one place for long. He had known that this could not continue. He had known he needed to find a place to wait out the storm, a place where he had no known associations. That's when he had thought of Jannie Bezuindenhout.

Jannie had grilled him about what had happened in Namibia before finally offering him a job at one of the ranches in Maputaland.

"Look, we are going to set you up at one of our properties along the coast, near St. Lucia Reserve," Jannie had said. "We haven't fully developed it yet, but you should be able to keep a low profile there. My partner will be back in town before too long, and we'll go over more details at that point. We're hiring you as a game manager, and this will give you a chance to get familiar with the land and animals."

When Jannie had dropped Malan off, he had left him with some basic supplies. "See you in a couple of weeks," Jannie had said as he got back into the truck and drove off.

"Fuck you," Malan had said to the retreating image of Jannie's truck vanishing into the bush.

And now here he was. He was glad to be back in the bush, and he knew he'd be nearly impossible to find as long as Jannie and his partner didn't turn him over. But if they had wanted to do that, they would have done it before bringing him out to Maputaland, Malan decided. Well, he would play along with them in the short term, as long as it suited his purposes.

The small village crossed his mind. He'd walked through it the day before and gotten sullen looks from behind partially closed doors. These people had no money and little prospects of ever having any. Their goats were their most valuable possessions, and it would be a rare day that they'd slaughter one for a meal. He'd spent the last two days hiking around the area. If he was going to be here a while, he wanted to know the landscape. There was plenty of game to be had, and the villagers would probably appreciate some fresh meat.

He reached for his rifle and started to walk. *Time to start building a new network.*

* * *

Pik Malan had been surprisingly open about the events at Sundowner Safaris when Jannie had pressed him. The world knew his crimes, and so there had been little point in trying to hide what couldn't be hidden. But he had made sure to state that he had not been responsible for the body.

Jannie and his partner drove up the coast to see him a few weeks later. Steven Reddman wanted to get the story straight from Malan. He also wanted to get a better idea of who Malan was.

Reddman pulled a cooler of cold beer out of the back of the truck and brought it over to the fire where Malan and Jannie were seated. He passed one to Malan, who took a deep swallow from the bottle.

"That's good, hey man," Malan said. "So what can I do for you gentlemen? I wasn't expecting company for a few days yet."

"We've come to talk about Namibia," Reddman answered, taking a beer for himself out of the cooler. He kept his face impassive, not wanting to show too much interest, but wanting to get straight to the point. "Jannie tells me there is a body buried at Sundowner Safaris?"

Malan stared at Reddman across the small fire. "Why are you so interested when there was no mention of one by the police or the reporter?"

"We have our reasons," Reddman replied. "Don't worry—it's not about you. It may have some relevance for an upcoming business deal."

"Whose body was it?" Jannie asked.

"I thought it was the journalist initially. After I got out of the country, I read the news reports and saw the photos of the police with the rhino horns, and I realized it wasn't her. Most probably it was one of my boys, a man named Edward. Not too intelligent and a nasty guy for sure, but he was useful in his own way. The journalist must have had help. No other way Edward ends up in that hangar burnt to a cinder. And the skull had a serious fracture on the side."

"There was no way to recognize the body when you found it?" Reddman asked.

"No. Everything burned except for the bones with a little charred flesh on them. The whole building was a wreck. They must have doused the whole place in aviation fuel to get it to burn like it did. Whoever it was wanted any evidence of them being there gone, and they did a good job of it."

Reddman listened to the man. Jannie was right about Malan. You could see he was born and raised in the African bush. His square jaw, tanned skin and big, lean frame spoke to a toughness bred of years in the wild. But Jannie was wrong about the man being stupid. He might look and play the rough Afrikaner farmer, but Reddman sensed a shrewd intelligence in the man's eyes and manner. You didn't rise to the top of the illegal wildlife trade like Malan had without some skill and vision.

Reddman knew that Malan was assessing him as well. There was no hint of fear in the man. Reddman had expected to find him nervous and jumpy. Instead, when they had driven up to the bungalow, he had been leaning back in his chair with his rifle next to him calmly roasting some warthog meat over the grill.

Reddman glanced at his brother-in-law. *You are the stupid one*, he thought. He was growing increasingly tired of the whole Bezuindenhout family—and that included Cecile. He still found Cecile beautiful, but that wasn't enough anymore. Their occasional lovemaking had become tired and routine, as was everything else in their relationship. He was pretty sure he had never loved her. He had married her for good reasons, but did he still need her or her family? The question intrigued him, but he knew the answer even as he asked it. The thought sent a spasm through his body, and he shivered.

"You getting a chill?" Malan asked. "Get closer to the fire, man."

Chapter 18

Matt glanced at Cecile on the truck seat beside him. Her thick, long, blonde hair was pulled back in a ponytail through the back of her blue baseball cap. But that only served to highlight the color of her eyes, her smooth, tanned skin and her soft, red lips. They were driving into the bushland that surrounded her family's old house to what she told him was one of her favorite places to look for game. The dirt track was partially grown over from lack of use, and the driving was slow. Cecile sat in the passenger seat, giving occasional directions while Matt slowly navigated the truck along the rutted path. On occasion, when she saw an animal, she would reach across and touch him lightly on the arm.

"Stop for a second. Look over there, beneath that small acacia tree. Do you see it?" Cecile asked, not taking her hand off his arm this time. Matt left his arm still, enjoying the smooth, warm touch of her hand.

At first, Matt didn't see anything. Then, as he kept looking, the small, golden shape of a serval emerged from the green grass, its large ears and eyes focused on the car.

"A serval. You've got sharp eyes to see that while we're bouncing along," he said.

"We call them tierboskat in Afrikaans. They are beautiful, aren't they?"

"Very beautiful."

"We're lucky to see one, as they are usually pretty hard to find in all this grass."

She squeezed his arm gently as the serval gave them one last look and slipped away. Matt put the truck back into gear, and they drove slowly off again. Cecile slipped her hand off his forearm and rested it on his thigh.

He'd been surprised when she'd flirted with him at breakfast. She had been so quiet at dinner the previous night that he had thought she wasn't happy to have a guest. But that had changed in the morning when the two of them had talked by the swimming pool. She had been friendly and forward, and he had liked it. After breakfast, he had returned to his room to get ready for their initial scout of the game at the farm. He had lain back on his bed for a moment and thought about Suzanne. The week between Christmas and New Year's Eve had been one of the best he could remember. He had gone into the office for a couple of days over the holidays, but they had spent the rest of the time together. Like Christmas, New Year's Eve had been spent with her parents. Matt couldn't remember being happier; but in the weeks since, things had changed. It had been subtle at first, and he had put it down to their busy work schedules. As time had gone on, she had become slower to return his calls and e-mails. The last call he had made was to tell her he was coming to Africa again for two weeks. She hadn't picked the phone up, and he'd left a message. She hadn't returned the call. She was pulling away from him, he realized, and there was little he could do.

"Stop here." Cecile glanced at him and smiled as she

stepped out of the truck and got her rifle off the rack. "From here, we go on foot," she said as she put on a pair of sunglasses.

Matt reached into the truck and grabbed his own rifle and camera.

They walked in silence for a mile, Matt following Cecile. The land was mostly rolling grassland broken with stands of acacia trees. They walked by a few gentle hills. It was quiet and still, but Cecile walked on, scanning the surrounding countryside. Matt knew how this day would end, and in truth, he wanted it to end that way as much as Cecile did. As she walked a few strides in front of him, he thought about Reddman. That he was married to Cecile was of no account. Over the years, Matt had slept with a number of married women, and any guilt he may once have felt about having an affair had long since been banished.

Out here, in the bush, looking for game, he wondered what surprises this trip would reveal. It was less than a day since he'd arrived, and the trip was already going in unexpected directions.

He was so deep in thought, that he didn't notice Cecile stop, and he almost walked into her. She was looking off into the bush.

"Do you see something?" Matt whispered to her.

"I thought I saw some movement, but perhaps not. Could just have been the breeze playing tricks."

Matt was standing right next to her now, and he put his hand around her waist and drew her to him. She didn't resist, pressing her back against his chest and turning her head sideways to kiss him. Her mouth opened as their lips touched, and she pressed more deeply against him. As their lips parted, she looked into his eyes. He saw a kindness and a need there, a need he wanted to fill.

"I've been thinking about that since you walked through the door yesterday," she whispered.

"Really?" Matt said, sliding his cheek against the side of her head. "That's good to hear."

"I just wanted you closer for a moment."

"Are we actually looking for game on this hike?"

Cecile laughed. "You don't think I'd bring you all the way out here under false pretenses, do you?"

She turned to face him, and they kissed again, this time more deeply than the first.

"We are almost there," Cecile said as she slowly pulled back, placing her free hand on Matt's chest. "It is good that we've established there is a mutual interest. It would have been silly wasting your two weeks here wanting each other but doing nothing about it, don't you think?"

"Very silly indeed."

With that, Cecile turned and walked on again.

"So, did you actually see anything in the bush, or did you just want to kiss me?" Matt asked.

Cecile glanced back at him and laughed again. "What do you think?"

They walked on for another fifteen minutes without seeing any animals. That didn't worry Matt, as he knew that hiking into the bush like this required patience. Wild animals rarely worked around people's schedules. That was part of the allure of the hunt: the search and the stalk.

As they came around the base of a gentle hill, a small stream trickled along the foot of a grass-covered slope that spread out before them. A thin row of acacia trees climbed the hill to their left.

Cecile stopped and put up her hand. Matt stopped behind her. She turned her head to him, put a finger to her lips and then pointed to the crest of the hill. Matt looked up the hill, and there, near the top, he saw a lone white rhino grazing its way across the slope. Moving slowly, they both walked towards the row of acacia trees. Once they were there, Cecile turned to Matt.

"You may want to get your camera out, as we're going to see how close we can get to him," she said.

"It's already out." Matt smiled. He slung his rifle over his shoulder.

"We are going to approach him along the line of trees, but we will go very slowly," she whispered. "We are downwind of him, so if we are careful, we should manage to get quite close. When we are near enough, I'll make a little noise, just enough to make him aware that he isn't alone. That should perk him up a bit, and you'll get some good rhino photos for sure."

"Sounds to me like you have done this before," he said.

"Many times when I was younger, but it has been a few years. You're not worried, are you?"

"Not at all." Matt grinned. "This should be fun."

They started up the hill slowly, Cecile in front, Matt behind. Every few strides she would stop, and they would crouch down and watch the rhino for a minute or two before proceeding. Cecile was right. Being downwind masked their scent, and that, coupled with their measured movements, was allowing them to get very close to the great animal without it noticing. It continued to graze, head down, cropping great mouthfuls of grass. A few red-billed oxpeckers hopped around on its back looking for ticks.

Cecile turned to Matt to see if he was ready with his

camera. He was already looking through the viewfinder and focusing on the rhino. She turned back to the animal and gave a sharp click of her tongue.

The reaction from the rhino was instant. Its head shot up, and its ears pointed directly at the tree they were under. Powerful bursts of air shot through the animal's nostrils as it scanned the tree line looking for the source of the noise, trying to catch a scent on the breeze. After a moment, the rhino trotted with surprising speed in a large arc that brought it further down the hill to a point where it was downwind of them. It stopped again, now catching their scent, and stood rigid, staring at the tree line. After a moment, it defecated, and then kicked the manure with its hind legs, spreading its pungent scent as it marked its territory.

Matt was taking pictures the whole time, Cecile standing quietly next to him, rifle in hand, keeping an eye on the rhino. They stood still for a few minutes while the animal remained alert and watchful. Then, apparently deciding they didn't pose a threat, the great beast returned to grazing, slowly making its way down the slope towards the small stream at the bottom.

"That was quite something," Matt said. "I think I got some great shots."

Cecile stepped closer and took his hand in hers, slipping her fingers between his. "They are beautiful animals in their own way, aren't they?"

"Yes, they are. Thank you for bringing me here."

"Come with me. We are almost there," she said as she gave his hand a pull.

They walked up along the remainder of the tree line to the top of the hill. On the far side of the hill, a smooth, rocky outcrop jutted out from the side of the hill, overlooking a small valley. A small herd of zebra grazed on the opposite slope, their tails flashing from side to side as they swatted at insects. Cecile walked over to the rocks and looked out across the valley.

"We are here," she said and took in a deep breath of air. "I used to come here years ago by myself and just sit here watching the animals as they came by. You see, over there, at the far end of the valley, there's a small water hole. It acts like a magnet to the animals, particularly in the dry season."

Matt put his gun and his camera down and walked up behind her. Slipping his hands around her waist, he pulled her close again. She tilted her head and allowed him to kiss her on the side of the neck as she dropped her hands and ran them over his arms. They stood for a moment, bodies close together, the valley spread out in front of them.

Cecile turned around in Matt's embrace and started to undo his shirt as she lifted her lips to his. He pressed against her as she started to take his shirt off, running her hands over his taut body as she did so. Matt took her baseball cap off and removed the band holding her hair. As her hair cascaded over her shoulders, he ran his fingers through it. Cradling her head, he kissed her more deeply.

She groaned with pleasure as he laid her down on the smooth surface of the rock, sliding into her with a smooth power that made her shudder. She lifted her head to his face and kissed him gently on the lips as he pressed into her. A spasm of pleasure shot through her body as she wrapped her legs around his, drawing him in more deeply as they melted into one another.

Later, they sat together on the rock, looking out over

the valley. Cecile had her back to Matt's chest and her arms draped over his legs. She was leaning gently against him.

"Thank you for that," she said. "I've needed to feel that for a long time now."

"You're welcome," Matt said.

"Do you have someone at home?" she asked.

Matt smiled. "Yes and no, I suppose."

"What do you mean by that cryptic response?"

"Well, there is someone. I've known her for over fifteen years, but she's pulling away at the moment. And she has the unfortunate habit of marrying other men, two of them since I have known her."

"Silly woman, if you ask me," Cecile said. "Don't give up on her, though, if you really do care. She probably is just afraid, especially if she's made mistakes before that have hurt her."

"Perhaps, but I can't wait on her all my life. We'll have to figure things out one way or another. And what about you? What brought you here to this rock to be with me?"

Cecile was quiet for a moment, though she started to caress his hand again. "This may sound silly, but I think I am ready for something different. I've been with Steven a long time now, but we are growing increasingly distant. I don't know that we ever actually loved one another, come to think of it. He's always been a driven man, but these last few years he has become increasingly obsessed with Genesis. Nothing else interests him. It might have been different if we had had children, I suppose, but that wasn't in the cards."

Matt sensed a certain sadness in her voice, and he held her more closely. "What would you like to do?" he asked.

"That's a good question. I'd like to simplify my life,

perhaps come here and help run the ranch. Take visitors out on game walks like we've just done. Well, maybe not exactly like what we've just done." She laughed.

"You might get more business that way." Matt smiled.

"Oh, you be quiet now. That will just be for special zoo guests from America with an interest in rhinos."

They sat silently for a time, enjoying each other's warmth and touch.

"I want to be around to help my father if he ever starts to slow down," Cecile said at last. Then her tone changed abruptly. "Steven is thinking of recruiting you to Genesis, you know." She turned her head to him. "He said you did some good work in Namibia."

"Really? I thought the work I did there was pretty superficial and poorly planned. The only thing that turned out right was the breakup of a poaching ring, and that wasn't really why I went."

"Why did you go?"

"To see if what Steven and Genesis were planning to do with the rhinos was feasible."

"And?"

"I left Namibia with more questions than when I arrived."

"And why have you come here? To see if you can find the answers to those questions?" Cecile asked while she continued to caress his hand.

Chapter 19

Steven Reddman stood on the small airstrip at Sundowner Safaris in northern Namibia. He had told Cecile that he and Jannie were going to take care of some business at a ranch in Limpopo. It had been a simple lie. The best lies usually were simple. She would be able to entertain Matt for a few days while he was away.

He had already checked the buildings at the center of the ranch when he had first driven onto the farm. The ranch lay abandoned. The main house was empty, the windows shuttered and the doors locked. He had walked around the buildings, checking out the possibilities and had liked what he had seen. He had considered suggesting to Tuhadeli that he acquire it as another game farm for his Damaraland operations.

The police had long since wrapped up their investigation. They had found nothing of use at the house or the burned-out hangar. Basking in the glory of a well-publicized raid and the breakup of a poaching ring, they had been content to conduct only a shallow investigation, taking their lead from the *Namibian Star*. Apart from arresting the local police captain, they had yet to track down any of the people involved in the ring.

The small airstrip and the burnt-out remains of the hangar seemed unremarkable when he went over to look at them. He tried to imagine what had happened the night the reporter had been rescued. He kicked at a few charred remnants under the blackened metal frame of a chair. *A man died here because of me*, he thought. *Did you do this, Matthew Harkes?*

He took the piece of paper out of his pocket and looked at the crudely drawn map. Then he got back into his truck and began driving. When he had gone about four miles, he stopped. A small kopje was just ahead, maybe a hundred yards away, rising over the bushland. He glanced at the map and read the directions again: near the base of a small kopje about ten yards away from a dead acacia tree, burnt black in a bush fire years earlier. He was in the right place, he was certain. He looked around, but didn't see any obvious signs indicating where Malan had buried the body. *I will have to look for it*, he thought.

As Reddman thought about what he might be about to find, an intense sensation came back to him. He remembered the feeling he had had in his San Diego office when he had first opened the box and seen the two skulls, their sightless eyes staring up at him. It was something he would never forget. Even now, he could feel the goose bumps rising on his arms.

Getting out of the cab, he reached into the back of the truck and pulled out the shovel. Sweat trickled down the back of his neck in the midday heat. He grabbed a handkerchief from his pocket and wiped some of it away. It was a futile gesture in this heat. He started to walk, looking from right to left as he searched for the burnt remains of an acacia tree. *A third skull*, he thought. Then he saw it, not fifty yards away—the blackened trunk of a dead acacia tree, its charred branches clawing at the blue sky.

Chapter 20

Cecile was brewing coffee for her father, who had just come in from the garden. It was early in the morning, and it still amazed her that he managed to get up with the sun every day.

"I've got too much to do," Samuel had said when she had suggested he might want to sleep in now and then. "Have you seen the state Boysen left the flowerbeds in at the entrance gates? It looks as if the place has been abandoned for weeks. God knows what people will think when they drive past."

She was making them both a cappuccino and turned the knob on the machine to the steam position as he walked into the kitchen. She picked up a small pitcher of milk and immersed the nozzle, slowly moving the pitcher around as the milk turned frothy.

"Two sugars in mine," Samuel said as he walked behind her and put his hands on her shoulders.

"The last thing you need, Dad, is more sugar." She smiled at him. "You're hard enough to deal with as it is."

Samuel smiled. "Your mother always thought that, as well."

He walked over to the kitchen table and sat down. He

looked at Cecile as she continued to froth the milk. "Is everything all right?" he asked.

He had noticed the change that had come over his daughter when Matt had arrived at the farm. She'd been tense with Steven the day before, but when Matt had arrived and then Steven had left for Limpopo, he had seen a deep sense of relief in Cecile, as if a weight had been lifted from her. In contrast, when she had returned from hunting with Matt, she had been laughing and smiling. It had been years since his daughter had seemed so happy.

"I want to leave Steven," Cecile said without turning away from the coffee machine.

Samuel sat silently for a few moments as she continued to make the coffee. "Have you told him yet?"

"No. It has been slowly dawning on me these past few weeks. I plan on telling him before this trip is over. I don't think I will be returning to America with him."

"You want to stay here at the farm?"

"Yes, if that's alright with you." Cecile brought both cups of coffee over to the kitchen table and sat down across from her father.

"Of course, it is," he said. "It will be nice to have you home again. This house will always be a home for you."

"That is not the only thing that has been bothering me," Cecile continued. "I suspect you noticed about Matt and me."

"It would be hard to miss—unless you weren't looking."

Cecile smiled. "Yes, I suppose it would be."

"Is it serious?"

"I don't really think so," she said, taking a sip of her coffee. "I just know it's something I've needed for a long time now."

"It is perhaps just as well that he has gone to Limpopo with Jannie for a few days," Samuel said." It will give you a chance to think things through. It will be a messy situation with Steven, you know. I don't think he is the type of man who will take you leaving very well."

Cecile thought for a moment. "Yes, I dare say it will be. But on some level, he must know that we are finished."

"That's not always the important thing. A man like Steven thrives on competition and possessions."

"You never really did like him, did you, Dad?"

"No, I can't say that I like him. But you were always attracted to men that I didn't approve of, and at the time he seemed the lesser evil." Samuel smiled as he spoke.

Cecile smiled back. "Yes, I suppose you're right. I did put you and mother through the meat grinder, didn't I?"

"That's just what all parents go through. I will be here for you through this, but you do have to take the lead in setting things right. And you do realize, even if Steven is reasonable on a personal level, with his and Jannie's business dealings being so intertwined, it is bound to get messy one way or another."

"That's another thing I wanted to talk to you about. Matt said some things the other night. You know he did some work for Steven in Namibia a couple of months ago, some work that involved black rhinos in Damaraland?"

"Yes, he told us about it the evening he arrived."

"Well, he also got involved in the breakup of that poaching ring in northern Namibia, the one that was all over the news as a result of the journalist being kidnapped and then escaping. You must have seen it in the papers."

"Yes, I may be getting on now, but I do keep an eye on the news."

"Before he left Namibia, the reporter told Matt some other things. Apparently the man who was Matt's contact in Namibia, a man named Jonathan Tuhadeli, is being investigated by the local paper for corruption."

"You could investigate half of Africa for corruption. In many ways, it is part of how business is done over here," Samuel said.

"Yes, I know. It seems this Tuhadeli is part of a company in Namibia called Ontstaan Properties, which is assembling a number of game ranches. There may be some corrupt land practices involved, but there are also suggestions that the company may be involved in the international rhino horn trade in some way."

"What are you saying?" Samuel said as he put down his coffee cup. "That Jannie and Steven might be involved in some sort of illegal activity?"

"I don't know, but the connection to Tuhadeli and to rhinos has me worried. I've never really taken too much of an interest in what Steven does. I've always known that Genesis works to conserve animals, but other than that I have no idea what he is involved in. Maybe he is getting involved to try to stop Tuhadeli. Or maybe he is implicated in some way. Either option would be extremely dangerous. But you know Steven. He likes to take risks. I wouldn't put anything past him. When he sets his mind on something, he doesn't let much stand in his way."

"Let's go for a walk around the garden and think about this," Samuel suggested." We have to protect the family when it comes down to it, but we can't do that if we don't understand what is happening. And I always think better outside in the fresh air. It tends to put things in perspective, I find."

Samuel stood up and put the coffee cup in the sink. "Don't worry about these. We can clean them up later."

Cecile walked out of the house behind her father, slipping her hand inside his elbow as they entered the garden. She liked having him close again. He had always been somebody she could confide in, even as a child.

"I think this could end up being a very messy situation," Cecile said. "But I am glad you're here to help."

Samuel had retired almost twenty years before, handing over the reins of the family's business interests to Jannie. Deeply involved with the running of the ranch in his time, Samuel had been a prominent member of the local community, serving on a wide range of charity boards. Since his retirement, he'd given up most of his community commitments, preferring to spend his time on and around the family's ranch.

"Do you really think Jannie would be involved in illegal activities?" Cecile continued. Deep down, she already knew the answer. Jannie was not her father, though he was similar in some ways. He was hardworking like their father, but lacked any real inspiration. He could be very committed to a project, but he was devoid of compassion. Perhaps most importantly, she knew, he possessed a taste for money, and he enjoyed the influence that went with it. Over the years, he had developed a deep working relationship with Steven. That had pleased Cecile initially, as she could see that Steven would be able to mentor her brother, but now she worried that Jannie was too much under Steven's thumb.

"Jannie is my own son, but he's not someone who I would turn to if I needed some moral guidance," Samuel said. "He might not be the one who thinks up various schemes, but if there is a profit to be made, I don't doubt he'd go along and adapt whatever the idea was to his own ends."

"He's probably followed along with whatever Steven has told him to do," Cecile said, frowning.

"Let's not jump to any conclusions. Just because a newspaper is doing an investigation doesn't mean there is anything illegal going on, let alone anything involving Jannie or Steven. We do have to protect the family, though, and that will be hard to do until we understand what is happening."

"How will we figure that out? Jannie isn't likely to fill us in even if we ask him. And Steven would be even harder to get a straight answer out of. Neither of them would take us seriously."

They walked on in silence, coming up on the bed of bush violets that her father planted for her each year. He knelt down and picked one.

"You know why I plant these every year, don't you?"

"It's because you remembered my favorite color is purple."

"That's part of it, yes. But it was also for myself, to remind me that this was your home, wherever life took you. I worked hard for a lot of years, and it was to make sure you and your brother would always have a place you could call home. So, the bush violets were for you, to make you feel special when you came home. But they were also for me while you were away, to remind me that while you weren't here, this was still your home."

"We have a decision to make here, don't we?" Cecile said.

"We do. You are right. I don't think Jannie or Steven are going to come out and tell us anything, even if we ask them. The question is: do you trust them? Do you trust Matt?" Samuel handed her the flower he had picked.

"My instincts tell me that whatever Steven and Jannie are doing, it could lead to trouble—and that would inevitably involve us. Matt, it seems to me, doesn't stand to gain anything here, at least not on a personal level."

"His relationship with Steven is just professional?"

"Yes. They just met a few months ago, after the rhino was slaughtered in Maryland."

"So, he's probably coming at this from the perspective of a conservationist?"

"Simple as that sounds, I think so," Cecile answered. "Dad, I think we need to look into this, even if it is just for our own sake. But how can we do that?"

"Come on. Let's walk back to the house. Jannie always leaves his office unlocked, and I suspect, with a little looking, we will be able to get a better idea of what might be going on."

The two walked back up to the house, again silent. Jannie's office was on the ground floor of the house. It had been Samuel's office until he had stepped back from the family business and let Jannie take it over. They walked down the hall and opened the door. The morning sunshine splashed though the window, lighting the whole room.

"Your brother greatly changed the room since I used to work in here. I don't know if you remember, but I used to have my hunting trophies on the walls. They have long since gone and have been replaced with all his war memorabilia from Angola."

As Samuel said it, Cecile sensed a tiredness in his voice, a sadness at the realization that he didn't fully trust his only son. "We don't have to do this, you know, Dad," she said.

A wan smile crossed his face. "There's a truth here that we don't know yet. It may be an ugly truth that neither of us really wants to discover, or it may be a good truth, but it is the truth, and we must find it."

Cecile lifted a photo off one of the bookshelves. It was a photo of Jannie many years before, when he was still in the army. He was standing next to a Buffel troop carrier in the bush, surrounded by other soldiers. They were all in their fatigues and bush hats, with guns slung over their shoulders, smiling for the camera. *He looks so happy here,* she thought to herself.

Samuel walked over to Cecile and looked at the picture as well. "He was happy in the army," he said. "But the Border War in Angola was such a tragedy. All those young men lost, and for what? We were on the wrong side of history there, fighting to prop up a system that was rotten to its core. Jannie has never accepted that, mind you."

"Yes, I know. I don't think he will ever accept it." Cecile put the photo back up on the shelf. "I suppose we'd better get started," she said, sitting down at the desk and turning on Jannie's computer.

"I'll look through the office filing cabinets and see if there is anything there of interest while you look through his computer," Samuel said, opening the top drawer.

Cecile waited for the monitor to warm up. "It requires a password," she said. "Any idea what Jannie might use as a password?"

Samuel stopped looking in the drawer. "It shouldn't be too hard to guess. I am sure it has something to with his time in the army."

"What was the name of his regiment?" Cecile asked.

"32 Battalion, the Buffalos."

She typed it in several ways. Each time failed. "No, I don't think that is it."

"Try the 'Terrible Ones.' It was how the battalion was known by the Angolans. I think Jannie has always been pleased that they earned that moniker."

"That did the trick. I'll give you one thing, Dad. You know your son."

"He is fairly predictable in some ways."

Cecile started to look through Jannie's computer while her father continued to rummage through the files. After an hour, neither of them had found much of interest.

"I didn't realize running a business could involve quite so much utterly boring material," she said as she opened another file under the sub directory "Ontstaan."

"Quite boring, I would agree. Have you searched using key phrases?" Samuel stepped away from the filing cabinet and sat down across the desk from Cecile. "Don't mind me. I just need to give my back a bit of a rest."

"Here's something that might be of interest," Cecile said, turning the monitor so her father could look without getting back up again.

"What is it?"

"It's a database titled 'Horn,'" she said as she opened it.

Samuel sat up, and they both looked at it.

"What is it?" Cecile asked.

"From what I can tell, it is an inventory of rhino horns at ranches across South Africa. It looks like a company called Ontstaan has been buying rhino horn. Some of these farms are either owned or managed by Ontstaan, but most of them are not."

"How can Ontstaan do that? Trade in rhino horn is illegal, isn't it?"

"Yes, it is—for the moment. Ranchers have been dehorning their rhinos for years to help protect the animals from poachers, but because they can't sell the horn, they have been stockpiling it. It looks like Ontstaan has been buying these stockpiles at well below the rate rhino horn sells for on the illegal market."

"Why would Ontstaan do that? And why would people sell it to them cheaply?"

"If I was guessing, it looks to me as if they are trying to corner the supply of South African rhino horn. I suppose the answer to the second part of the question is simple: money in the pocket. Farmers have long wanted to sell the stuff, but even limited trade has been illegal for decades. By selling cheaply now, they are getting at least some return on their investment. Ontstaan is obviously gambling that it will be able to sell the horns at some point for a higher price."

"But what does Ontstaan have to do with Jannie and Steven? Why does Jannie have so many files about Ontstaan? Are they just trying to figure out what Ontstaan is doing?" Cecile asked.

Samuel leaned back in his seat. "I don't know. Maybe the answer is somewhere in these files. We'll just have to keep looking."

Chapter 21

Jannie pulled the truck up outside the house, and Matt got out of the passenger door with his rifle and backpack. Reddman stepped through the front doorway of the house and walked over to shake Matt's hand.

"Welcome to Maputaland," Reddman said. "I'm afraid this place isn't quite as well kept as the family house in Kwa-Zulu Natal, but I think we will manage."

Matt looked at the house. It was a one-level, red brick structure with a thatched roof. The garden was overrun with weeds, and the windows looked in need of a good wash.

"We just bought this place three months ago," Reddman said turning around and looking at the house. "The idea is to refurbish the house, install a campsite with bungalows and see if we can't draw some of the tourist traffic that goes to Mkuzi. If that doesn't work, we will look to turn it around and sell it to an investor. In the meantime, the facilities are fairly rudimentary."

"Don't worry about me on that count," Matt said. "When I am out in the country, I prefer to rough it."

"Excellent! Too much comfort can make a man soft, don't you agree?" Reddman asked. "At any rate, I don't expect you will be spending too much time inside in the coming week."

Jannie got back into the truck, started the engine and drove off with a curt wave through the window.

"Where is he off to?" Matt asked.

"He's gone to get the gentleman who will be your hunting guide. Someone we've just hired as a game manager. He's been out in the bush surveying the farm for us and getting a better idea of the game we have and what we might need to purchase. Let me tell you, this guy likes to live rough as well. He was born and bred under an African sky for sure."

"Sounds like quite a character," Matt replied.

"He certainly is. But let's get inside and get settled. I want a quiet chat with you before they get back. I imagine Jannie will be gone for a couple of hours."

They both walked to the front door of the house and went inside.

"You weren't kidding, were you?" Matt said as he looked around the room. The walls were bare, and the only furniture that remained in the living room was a worn couch and a couple of wooden chairs. The kitchen was much the same, except that there were no chairs. There was a pool out back, but the water was stagnant and filled with garden debris.

Reddman smiled. "Well, as I said, it is a work in progress. When we have finished with it, you won't be able to recognize it. Let's unpack, and then we can chat out back while we wait for the other two to arrive."

"Sounds good," Matt said. He picked up his backpack and rifle.

Reddman pointed down the hallway. "Pick any of the rooms. They are all pretty basic."

Matt walked into the first room on the left and threw his backpack onto the end of the bed. He took his rifle out of its case and checked the gun. The hunting had been good with Cecile. He had shot a trophy kudu buck, and Cecile was going to have the horns mounted for him. The nyala was more challenging. Although they had seen a number of animals, none were trophy animals, and they had passed on taking one.

"Never mind," Cecile had said on the final drive back to the house. "You will just have to visit again."

He smiled at the memory as he slipped the rifle back into its case. The thought appealed to him. He walked out to the back porch, where he found Reddman sitting in an old garden chair.

"Sit down and let's talk," Reddman said.

Matt pulled up a chair and sat down.

"Do you know why I invited you back to Africa?"

Matt was quiet for a moment. "I assume it wasn't just because you wanted a hunting companion."

Reddman laughed. "No, not at all. To get to the point, I want to recruit you to Genesis. I need you to be my representative to the zoos in North America. The whole idea of basing the conservation of a species like rhinos on frozen zoos has been a hard sell. I have been pushing this for a number of years now, but people are tired of hearing it from me. What I need is a fresh voice, an industry insider, to be the face of this effort. I need a respected rhino expert from the zoo industry to convince the zoos to get on board. And I think Matthew Harkes is that man."

"That's very flattering, Mr. Reddman," Matt said, "but I don't know. I'm not sure that public relations is my strength."

"It's not all public relations, although that is part of the job. More than that, in Genesis, I need people who can take action when required and who show personal initiative when it is needed. And you showed both traits while in Namibia. I'll be honest with you. You weren't my first choice to come to Africa, but Natalie convinced me that you could do the job—and she was right. An amazing woman, Natalie."

"Yes, she is," Matt replied. He started to say something else, but Reddman cut him off quickly.

"Before you say anything else, you need to hear out my idea. There's a lot about Genesis that you don't yet know, and if you are to come on board, you need a clear idea of what we are looking to achieve."

Matt leaned forward in his chair. "You're looking to build an effective conservation model for endangered species, starting with the rhino, correct?"

"That's part of it, but it's more than that. You know about the North American side of the business, the side I want you to be involved in, but you don't yet know about the Asian side of our business model."

Matt noticed Reddman reach down and finger a small sports bag he had placed next to his chair. "The Asian side of the business?"

"Yes, perhaps the most profitable part of the business model—in reality, the revenue stream that supports a great deal of what we do."

Reddman continued to finger the bag and smiled at Matt. "It is the part of the business that requires people who are willing to take risks and do what is required for the good of the company."

"Exactly what are you talking about?" Matt asked.

"I'll cut to the chase, Matt. Genesis trades in rhino horn with a variety of suppliers in Vietnam, Thailand and China. We've been doing it for years."

"You have to be kidding me. That's illegal under international law. Why on earth would you think I would be party to something like that?" Matt said, stunned by Reddman's sudden admission.

"Hear me out before you make any judgment," Reddman said. "First, let me tell you a story about how I got involved in all of this. I think I told you that during the Vietnam War I served in Saigon, assigned to the military police. It was there that I first got involved in business. It started with the simple arrest of a man who was running a prostitution operation. He offered me money to let him go. I knew that arresting the man wouldn't have done any good anyway. There was no way we could shut down prostitution in the city, there was too much of it, and so I took the money. Word quickly spread that I was an American with whom the locals could do business. It wasn't too long before the local syndicates contacted me and said they wanted to work with me on an ongoing basis. I agreed, and pretty soon I was skimming a lot of money off the local prostitution, drug and gambling trade. That money provided the foundation for my future wealth.

"I loved Saigon and might even have stayed there if the war hadn't been lost. I left with the other troops. But later on, as travel restrictions to Vietnam relaxed, I went back for a visit and reconnected with the people I had been working with during the war. The Vietnamese were running protection rackets throughout the city, and these involved an extensive network of traditional medicine shops. People could buy everything from rhino horn to sun bear gall bladders. The belief in the value of traditional remedies ran deep. There were also growing signs of wealth in the city, with more people acquiring Western-style clothing, motorbikes and cars. I still remember the moment I realized the potential of the market. I paid a visit to a traditional medicine shop in what was by then called Ho Chi Minh City. A young couple walked in and bought a small packet of powdered tiger bone. What struck me wasn't the purchase, as I had already known about the illegal trade in wildlife. Rather, it was that the couple was so young, they still held to the traditional beliefs and they had the money to make the purchase.

"I had already married Cecile by that time and was in the process of becoming a partner with Jannie in the game farm here, after Samuel retired. As a result, I had access to a steady supply of rhino horn. The Vietnamese saw rhino horn as a profitable side business, but I saw a larger opportunity. What was needed was an increase in demand, something to drive the price higher. Rhino horn was used as a cure for headaches and minor pains. Like tiger bone, it could be ground into powder and sold in small packets. There was a steady demand for it, but I realized that with a little rebranding, I could put it on a path of explosive growth. That was where I got the idea. Using the syndicates' influence over the traditional medicine shops, we planted a rumor that rhino horn cured cancer. The rumor spread like wildfire, and demand quickly outstripped supply, driving the price of rhino horn to levels even I had not imagined. As a result, we were able to expand our markets into other parts of Southeast Asia and China. The Chinese market alone is enormous."

Matt was shocked. "But you have set Genesis up as a

conservation effort. You have said that you are trying to save the rhinos, not kill them for their horns."

"The goals are not mutually exclusive," Reddman said evenly. "The trade in rhino horn and other traditional medicines has been going on for centuries, and it will continue to go on for many more centuries. There is nothing you or I can do to stop it. But we can manage it. Think about this. If the rhinos are all killed off, then the rhino horn business will die with them. So, the people who are making huge profits from the sale of rhino horn are the people who have the greatest interest in making sure that rhino continue to thrive. Trade in rhino horn has been illegal for decades, but the laws have failed to preserve the species. People need to realize that the only way to save endangered species is to place a value on them, to turn them into a commodity, just like any other good or service that is bought, sold and traded. Conservation organizations, zoos included, have tried to take the high road with this for years, and they are failing. You know it is true. You are on the front lines. Think about the pressure on the rhino population now, and that is only going to grow in the coming decades as Asia really comes into its own."

"But what you are talking about is illegal," Matt objected. "And where do you get the horn?"

"Don't be naïve, Matt. We hunt rhino here in South Africa on a variety of ranches and in national parks. Sometimes we use the hunting permit system. Other times we stage the killings as poaching incidents. But the poaching is just the tip of the iceberg. That is to whet the appetite of the markets in Asia and to help set up reliable distribution networks. We are currently the dominant supplier of rhino horn to all the major traditional medicine markets, and that will only grow. We've also been purchasing stockpiled rhino horn from ranches around the country. They have been legally dehorning their animals for decades to foil the poachers, and we are quietly buying it all at bargain basement prices. We will shortly have a virtual monopoly on all the rhino horn in sub-Saharan Africa."

"Why are you telling me this?" Matt asked. "I could just as easily go to the police as I could agree to join you."

"I've taken a calculated risk telling you this, that's true enough. But right now, it would just be your word against mine. And you've already helped expand the reach of Genesis with your work in Namibia. You removed a major competitor there, and you were quite brutal about it, weren't you?"

"What are you talking about?" Matt's mind raced back to his time in Ruacana.

"I am talking about killing a man, Matt. I'm talking about hitting a man so hard you fractured his skull." With that, Reddman reached into the bag next to his chair and pulled out the charred skull he had dug up in Namibia. "This, I believe, Matthew Harkes, was your work. I dare say you don't recognize the man. After all, it has been almost three months since you last saw him."

Matt stared at the skull. He could see the fractures along the right side by the temple where his rifle had slammed repeatedly. If Patrick hadn't pulled him away, it would have been worse.

"Was this your first kill, Matt?" Reddman continued. "I remember mine vividly. It was in Vietnam when I was in the military police. It wasn't part of the war. The man was a shopkeeper who sold traditional medicines and other items. He was a fool. He had refused to pay a protection fee and then encouraged other small businesses to do the same. Along with two other MPs who helped me run the neighborhoods, I arrested him late one night. We took him deep into the countryside and beat him to death. It was a deeply satisfying experience. It sent a message, and all the other business owners from that point on paid our fee willingly."

"But I didn't think of keeping the skull then," Reddman continued. "That practice was inspired by a story Jannie told me years ago. We were swapping war tales on a safari at one of the game ranches. Cecile had retired to the lodge after dinner, leaving Jannie and me to share a bottle of single malt whiskey around the fire. It was a cool night, and we were enjoying the heat of the fire and the whiskey. That's when Jannie told me about Operation Protea in Angola in 1981. The objective had been to clear SWAPO's northwest headquarters out of the Angolan town of Xangongo, and 32 Battalion, Jannie's unit, had been at the forefront of the action. Jannie had been in the thick of the fighting and had killed several of the terrorists. He described each kill in great detail, but one of those stories struck a chord and stayed with me. After the week-long battle, the Battalion had displayed a trophy skull of a SWAPO soldier killed in the fighting. The man had died so quickly, the skull still had chewing gum between its teeth."

Matt said nothing. His eyes were fixed on the skull.

"You look a little ill," Reddman said as he turned the skull so the eye sockets were facing Matt. "Funny that there was no mention of this in the media. You have two choices here, Matt. You can walk away from my offer to work for Genesis, but if you do, rest assured that your career will be destroyed and you will probably serve time in a Namibian prison. That is choice one. Choice two is to come and work for Genesis, be incredibly well paid for your efforts and at the same time play a key role in building a model of conservation that actually works."

Reddman was right. Matt did feel sick to his stomach. The skull was a stark reminder of what had happened in Ruacana. His mind was racing. Reddman had deduced what had happened in the hangar, but how? *Shit, he knows I killed a man, and he's using it to blackmail me.*

"What do you want me to do?" Matt asked cautiously.

Reddman gave him a searching look, but Matt remained guarded, his face passive.

"What I want you to do is to be the North American face of Genesis," Reddman answered. "At the moment, there are two facets to Genesis: the legal trade in rhino genetic material and the currently illegal trade in rhino horn. I need a respected zoo professional with extensive experience with rhinos to oversee and grow the legal operation. You don't need to worry about the horn side of the operation, as I have another man to help me with that. And don't get too hung up on the illegal aspect of what we are doing. Sooner rather than later, the rest of the world will come to the realization that the only way to save endangered species is to trade in them. When that happens, Genesis will be well placed to dominate the trade and, in doing so, save a wide range of species. Rhinos are just the beginning."

"So, what you had me go to Namibia for is actually a genuine part of the legal business?"

"Very much so. We need to get the zoo community to rethink how they manage their breeding programs, to move away from the model of importing animals and live breeding to the model of the frozen zoo. Once that has been achieved, Genesis will be well placed to dominate that trade as well."

Matt leaned back in his chair, still looking at the skull that Reddman was idly fingering as he spoke. *This man must be half crazy*, he thought. *Where did he get the skull from?* Matt remembered Silke lying prone on the ground, about to be raped, and the flash of rage that had led him to kill the man. It had all happened so quickly, but he knew he would do it again. With that realization, he felt a hardening of his resolve. Reddman was right. Matt was a man who could take action when required and who was not afraid to take risks, even break the rules if it led to a good result in the end. He knew he had to keep listening.

They talked for another hour, discussing the zoo market in North America and the role that Genesis could play in building genetically viable populations of collection animals, as well as supporting viable populations in the wild. Matt kept finding himself glancing back to the skull. Reddman never stopped touching it, his fingers slowly moving over its surface. *You are crazy*, Matt thought. *I'm talking to a mad man*. But he was also aware that it was he and not Reddman who had killed the man in the hanger.

A truck door slammed, quickly followed by another.

"I think Jannie is back with our other guest," Reddman said as he stood. He placed the skull carefully on the armrest of the chair.

Matt stood up as Jannie came through the house, followed by a man in a bush hat. There was something familiar about the man, though Matt couldn't initially place him.

"Pik, good to see you again," Reddman said. "Let me introduce you to Matthew Harkes. Matthew, this is Pik Malan."

Malan stepped towards Matt and held out his hand. "Good to meet you, man."

"Pik Malan?" Matt said and looked at Reddman in disbelief.

"Is there a problem?" Malan asked.

"Not at all. It's just that the two of you have crossed paths before," Reddman said.

Malan looked at Matt. "I don't believe we've met before," Malan said. "I remember faces, and yours is one I haven't seen before."

"No, you haven't. But the two of you have had dealings with each other in Namibia," Reddman said. "Matt is the man who rescued the reporter from your ranch in Namibia."

Malan glared at Matt. "You burned the hangar down and killed one of my men? You're the reason I am a wanted man in my own country?"

Matt met his glare without flinching. "Yes, that was me. But you're a wanted man by your own hand, not mine."

"Now, gentlemen, relax for a moment," Reddman intervened. "We can't have you two getting off on the wrong foot if we are all going to work together." A faint smile crossed his face.

Jannie, leaning against the door frame, was also grinning as he watched the confrontation between Matt and Malan. "Anyone for a cold beer?" he asked and then turned to go back into the house.

Everyone was quiet for a moment. Then Malan said, "Ja, why not? What is done is done." He glared at Matt again and then looked at Reddman. "Why is he here?"

Then Malan glanced at the skull on the armrest, seeing it for the first time. "What's that?" he asked.

"Don't you recognize your own man?" Reddman

asked. "This is what is left of your friend Edward, recently imported from Namibia. Don't look so aghast, Pik. Why do you think I asked you where you buried the body?"

Malan started to say something, but the words seemed to stick in his throat.

"Sit down, gentlemen," Reddman ordered. "There is much for us to discuss."

Jannie came back out of the house and passed each of them a beer. "Everyone settled down a bit, hey? Good. Now let's get down to business."

"You are both here for a reason," Reddman said. "I've just been talking with Matt about him joining Genesis and overseeing our North American operation." He started to stroke the skull again.

"Pik," Reddman continued, "your crimes are widely known, particularly since your operation in Namibia blew up courtesy of our mutual friend Matt here." He nodded towards Matt, who was still staring at Malan. "Yours is a simple choice. We will help you remain off the radar screen of the authorities and pay you a generous amount to run our sub-Saharan rhino horn operation. As you know, we want to expand into Zimbabwe, Zambia and Mozambique—and rhinos are just the start of it. Because of your unique skill set and your contacts in the region, we can use you despite the baggage you bring."

"Fair enough," Malan said, as he continued to stare at the skull Reddman was handling. "I'm in."

"And you, Matt, what do you say? Your choice is as simple as Pik's. You're either in, or we will do everything in our power to discredit and ruin you. If you're in, however, we'll work towards some mutual goals, and you will end up far richer than you could ever expect to be from working in the zoo industry back in the States."

Matt glanced at the skull and then at Malan. He lifted the bottle of beer to his lips and took a deep drink. "I'm in as well," he said, putting down the beer bottle.

"Great. Welcome aboard, gentlemen. There will be one thing you have to do before you come into Genesis, though. I've told you a great deal about what we do, perhaps not all the details, but you now have a pretty good idea of the scope of Genesis. But you will have to show your commitment to the company. Matt, you wanted to hunt in Africa. Well, now you will have the chance. You and Pik will go into Mkuzi Game Reserve and poach a rhino. I want the horns by the end of the week."

Chapter 22

"You realize that Reddman is out of his mind," Matt said to Malan.

They were on foot, hiking into Mkuzi Game Reserve. Malan walked in front, rifle casually slung over his shoulder. Matt walked behind, with his gun in his hand. The two of them had hardly spoken on their drive out to Mkuzi. It was a gray, overcast day. The ground was wet from the previous night's rain.

"Ja, that is fairly obvious. Anyone who digs up the dead has some issues to deal with," Malan answered. He paused for a moment in front of a pile of rhino dung, and then walked on, his eyes flashing to the left and right as he looked for other signs. "That shit is at least two weeks old, but at least we know there are rhino in the area."

Matt glanced at the dung as he walked by and found himself agreeing with Malan's assessment. *Being able to age rhino dung is a funny thing to have in common with a man like this,* he thought. Matt had been trying to figure a way out of killing a rhino since Reddman had sprung the condition on him. The thought of shooting an endangered species sickened him. This would serve no purpose other than to show his commitment to Reddman and Genesis and add a criminal element to his own involvement. That is, of course, what Reddman wanted, to draw him more deeply into the Genesis fold, to bind him to the company.

"So, why did you kill my man Edward and burn the hangar down in Ruacana?" Malan asked while continuing to walk. He didn't look at Matt as he asked the question.

Matt thought for a moment before answering. Malan was a violent man, and Matt quietly unclipped the safety on his rifle. He remembered how close he'd come to being shot by Malan in Damaraland. He would have been long dead by now but for Patrick's intervention.

"I could ask you why you had a female reporter kidnapped and beaten, lying naked on the hangar floor with your man standing over her about to rape her," Matt said. The memory of what Silke had been put through angered him, but he knew it wasn't the time to provoke a confrontation with Malan. "Not that it makes any difference now, but I didn't mean to kill the man, just knock him out. It was a flash of anger."

Malan walked on, his rifle still slung over his shoulder, deep in thought. "That's fair enough," he said. "I might have killed him myself if I'd known what he was up to. A nasty guy, but he had his uses. And you can put the safety back on that rifle of yours. I have no intention of killing you, at least not today."

Matt smiled but didn't touch the safety. "Can't be too careful in Africa, I've found. Too many crazy people about for that."

"Don't worry. I am many things, but crazy is not one of them."

They walked on for a bit in silence.

"What I don't understand is how you found us in

Ruacana," Malan said, stopping and turning to Matt. "Not even the reporter knew where we were. It was the stupid police captain who panicked, kidnapped her and brought her to the ranch. How did you know where to look?"

"Ruacana wasn't the first place I crossed your path," Matt replied. "I had come across a rhino carcass in Damaraland the week before Ruacana and was tracking the people who did it. You were waiting on a hill to shoot me, and I suppose you would have if I hadn't been warned at the last minute."

"You spotted me on the hill?"

"With the help of a friend who was there to help me find the rhinos. He was an ex-SWAPO fighter and familiar with the trap you set."

For the first time since he had met him, Matt saw a grin spread across Malan's face. "Damn guerrillas! They made life difficult in the war, but who can blame them? It is their country, after all. Was it you bastards who drained my water that day?"

"That was my friend's idea. We wanted to get you away from the area."

Malan laughed. "It worked! I wondered about that for days. That water can didn't leak, and I couldn't find any tracks about. Your friend has got some bush talents, hey. That was a thirsty drive home. If my truck had broken down, I might have been in trouble. When I get back to Namibia, might be I should hire this SWAPO friend of yours."

Matt looked at Malan, surprised. "I don't think he'd be interested in the kind of work you do."

"I wouldn't bet on that. As you know, with the right motivation, most men will do surprising things."

"Would you have shot me if I'd come around the base of the hill on those tracks?" Matt asked.

"Ja, probably," Malan said. "What did you think I was waiting there for? It would just have been business." He looked intently at Matt. "Don't take it personally. I was just protecting my investment. Where I shot that rhino, it wasn't too likely that anyone would have come across it in the time I was on the hill. I would have been surprised to see you, but yes, I would have shot you."

After a moment of silence, Matt said, "I wasn't the first man to track you to that hill."

Malan looked hard at Matt, appraising him. "No, there was another. But I didn't shoot him from the hill. He had been close enough to hear the shots when I killed the rhino. We had gone only a short distance into the bush before we heard him coming after us. We took him alive because we needed him to talk. The man was brave, I'll give him that, but eventually he talked. Not that he had much useful information. Just that a local SWAPO character named Jonathan Tuhadeli had hired him and sent him to track down the poachers. I told you Edward had his uses. He helped me work the man over. He even snuffed cigarettes out on the man's face. He enjoyed what he was doing. For me, it was just business. A message needed to be delivered, and this was the most emphatic way to send it. It was Edward who drove the body to Khorixas and dumped it in the street."

"You had two vehicles?"

"Ja. The other vehicle was equipped for animal transport. If anybody asked, we were in Damaraland to pick up some game animals I had bought from another ranch." Malan paused. "I stayed behind on the hill just in case the first man had a partner. I thought the first body would be enough to scare people off, but I wasn't taking any chances."

"I didn't know about the body," Matt said. "My ex-SWAPO friend didn't tell me about it until later."

They had begun walking again, but this time side by side. "Now let me ask you another question," Malan said. "What are you doing here in Africa with a character like Reddman?"

"That's a good question. You might be surprised, but he is actually a respected businessman back home in the States, with some deep roots in the conservation world. I first came over to do him a favor in Damaraland, to do a preliminary survey of what it would take to collect genetic material from the rhino population in northern Namibia."

"And that's how you got on my trail?"

"Yes, that's right. I had never heard of you until after we drained your water that day. We took your license plate number as well and were able to get our contact in Khorixas to track it to the ranch in Ruacana."

"Your contact was Tuhadeli?"

"Yes," Matt answered.

"That makes sense," Malan said. "I wonder if he even had to look up the license plate number or if he already knew who I was."

Matt wondered how much he dared to tell Malan. "Apparently, Tuhadeli is involved in a big land deal in Namibia, setting up a series of game ranches with some Chinese backers."

Malan nodded. "Ja. He probably saw my operation as competition, and that's why he wanted you to track me down. He is a ruthless man, Tuhadeli."

They were walking up the side of a bush-covered hill.

Malan stopped and sat down on a rock. Pulling a piece of biltong out of his backpack, he offered it to Matt.

Matt took it and bit off a piece of the dried, salty meat. "This is pretty good," he said, chewing.

"Ja, not bad stuff when you are hungry and in the bush." Malan chewed for a moment. "So why did you come after me by yourself and not report what you found to the police?"

"Reddman's contact, Tuhadeli, had been telling me that the police might be involved. That, I think, was a just a ruse to stop me from going to the authorities. But given what the police officer in Ruacana did to Silke, maybe he wasn't too far off the truth."

"So you came after me yourself? You and this guerrilla friend of yours?"

"That's right. It seemed the right thing to do at the time."

"You know Reddman and Jannie tried to buy me out last year? They wanted me to work for them, to use my contacts to help them take over more of the rhino trade in southern Africa."

"No, I didn't know that, but given what I've learned since, it doesn't surprise me."

"My Asian contacts got in touch with me saying that some South African colleagues wanted to meet with me. So, I flew to Johannesburg and met Jannie and Reddman in a steak house in Sandton. Reddman told me that if we merged our operations, we could reduce our costs, ensure more efficient distribution and expand our markets. Instead of competing against one another, we could create a monopoly and be better able to control the price."

"It makes sense," Matt agreed. "But you turned them down?" It was a question.

"Ja. My operation was running well, I was making a good profit, and I didn't particularly want to work for someone else."

"So, I suppose I did them a favor in Namibia, didn't I?" Matt asked.

"I'll say you did. Reddman isn't the type of man to take no for an answer. If you don't join him, he will shut you down and force you to join him."

"You're not upset about that?"

"Ja, but what can I do? It's business. I'll still make a lot of money working for Reddman, so for now I'll go along. It will be a while before I can go back to my own country anyway." Malan said. "But things will eventually calm down. They always do."

Malan stood up and started walking up the hill again. "Come on. We've got to keep moving if we are going to find that rhino of yours. They are here in the park, but I haven't seen any fresh sign of one yet."

Matt stood up and followed. His boots were soaked from the wet grass and muddy ground, but he preferred this to hunting in the heat and humidity.

"You didn't really answer my question," Malan said. "I know why you were in Namibia, but why have you come back to South Africa? You don't seem like the type of man who wants to be involved in this sort of work."

Matt hesitated. "I like to hunt. Reddman invited me to come and hunt on his game farm. Reddman is working on a business deal with my boss, so it was a good political move to come."

Malan grunted. "You can't say Reddman didn't hold up his end of the bargain. You're getting an opportunity to hunt."

The two of them walked on for another mile before Malan stopped and knelt down. They had come to a game path that cut through the deep, wet grass. A large pile of fresh rhino dung sat to one side.

"This is much more recent," Malan said. "Perhaps within the last hour or two, I'd guess. And see the tracks? I'd say we have a large male white rhino that has been through here this morning."

Matt knelt down next to Malan. This was what he'd been hoping not to find. He wanted more time to find a way out of shooting the rhino, but Malan was good at what he did.

"I shouldn't think he's gone too far, and he will be easy to track in this wet ground." Malan said. "I think we will have your horn by lunch time."

Matt frowned. He realized Malan was right. The rhino was most likely within a mile or two of where they now stood, probably closer. On a cool day like this, it would be taking its time grazing. With a skilled hunter like Malan tracking it on soft ground, it was as good as dead already.

The rhino was closer than Matt had thought, and they found it within ten minutes. Malan was right. It was a large male white rhino with two spectacular horns. They were downwind of the animal, but it was grazing its way across a gentle grass-covered plain. The grass was tall enough that Matt could not see the animal's legs. Occasionally, it would lift its head, chewing a mouthful of grass, and turn its head from side to side to survey its surroundings.

Malan touched Matt on his shoulder and indicated they should walk in a large arc around the animal, using some bushes for cover. That way, they could come at it from the side, where Matt would be able to get a kill shot.

Matt nodded his head, and they started carefully walking, always keeping an eye on the great animal. Matt could tell it was an animal in its prime. He thought back to the white-tailed buck in Maryland he had wanted to cull from the herd. That animal had already passed its genes on to the next generation, and the herd would be healthier with its passing. This rhino was different. It was an animal that should also have the chance to breed, but he was minutes away from bringing it down forever. But there was no way out of this. *When the time comes,* he thought to himself, *at least do it right. Don't hesitate, and make it a good, clean shot.*

The rhino continued its slow progress across the plain, grazing contentedly, secure in its size.

When they were abreast of the animal, Malan came to a stop. They were standing under a tree with a low branch that Matt could use to rest his rifle on and steady his aim. Matt set himself up for the shot.

"I see you left the safety off," Malan whispered as Matt started to aim.

Matt gave him a quick sideways glance. "As I said, this is Africa, and there are some crazy people about."

He looked back down the telescopic sight on his rifle. The rhino loomed large in it. The moisture from the grass had painted the lower part of the animal's body a dark gray, while the dry upper half remained lighter. He moved his scope along the line formed by the moisture until it came to the point right behind the shoulder, the kill spot. Until that point, he hadn't put his finger on the trigger, but now it moved there with the ease that comes from long practice. He started to press gently against it, but suddenly the rhino vanished from the scope, and the barrel of the gun lifted up.

Matt looked up from the scope. It was Malan. He had been standing next to Matt while he had lined up his shot, but now his hand was on the barrel of the gun, and he'd lifted it up to the sky.

"What are you doing?" Matt asked in a low voice. "That was a kill shot."

"The rhino can wait. You still haven't given me a good answer as to why you are here in Africa with Reddman. You're not the sort of man who would normally come out and poach a rhino, and I don't think that you want so much to work for Genesis, not given what you do for a living and what you now know about the company. I can see that he might be trying to blackmail you with Edward's death, but you and I know that is weak and wouldn't stand up in court. Even if it did, you would have the newspapers and public opinion on your side for what Edward was trying to do to your reporter friend. And any attempt Reddman made to go public with the skull would put the spotlight on him. So I ask myself, what are you here for, Matt, and why are you willing to kill this animal?"

"You're not the gruff Boer farmer people take you for, are you?" Matt asked.

"People see what they want to see," Malan said. "But I wouldn't have lasted as long as I have if I wasn't good at reading people. You have a different agenda here."

Matt leaned against the branch of the tree and looked back at the rhino, still grazing quietly. He was silent for several moments. Then, he said, "I want to get into Genesis so I can do to it what I did to your organization in Namibia. To bring it down, I need to be on the inside. The reporter who I rescued and who did the story in Namibia is now at the *Herald* here in South Africa. The newspaper is already investigating the rhino horn trade, including the possible role of Reddman and Genesis in that, but they need more evidence to publish the story. They asked for my help. That's why I am here."

"You want to bring Reddman down? Why should I let you do this?"

"Whether I succeed or not, with a major news organization looking into it, Reddman's operation is going to come under the spotlight sooner rather than later. Better to be on the side that is bringing it down than the one that is propping it up. And I can't imagine that you are interested in any more media coverage."

"This is true. I have no intention of helping Jannie and Reddman. I just want to use them as a cover so I can lie low for a while. There is no chance that I will use my contacts to help Genesis. It seems we are both playing a similar game with Reddman."

"It would seem so," Matt agreed. He brought his rifle back to bear on the rhino, which had hardly moved during his exchange with Malan. "And this is my ticket inside."

Again the gun barrel lifted.

"There is no need to shoot this animal," Malan said. "I will give you the horns you need to get into Genesis—on two conditions. I have the horn stored in a village near the bungalow."

"You've already poached rhino here?"

Malan shrugged his shoulders. "It is what I do."

"Why would you give me the horns? What are the conditions?"

"The first you will already do. That is to bring down Reddman and Genesis. The second is to leave out any mention of me in any investigation that follows. I like

Maputaland and would like to stay here for a while, but I won't be able to do that if people are looking for me."

Matt looked at the rhino again. It was now slowly walking away from them. He knew Malan was a man who would reestablish his poaching operation quickly, especially with Genesis and Reddman out of the way. *Genesis is the bigger problem here, and making this deal will buy some time for the rhinos,* he reminded himself. *And it will save me from shooting this beautiful animal.* He held out his hand to Malan.

"That's a deal."

* * *

"Amazing," Reddman said. "I wasn't sure you'd go through with it."

"I told you I was in, didn't I?" Matt said. He was relieved he had not had to shoot a rhino himself, but still a rhino had been killed to pay his entry fee into Genesis. He watched as Reddman ran his hands over the two horns.

"Ja, and it was a great shot," Malan said, slapping Matt on the shoulder. "The rhino dropped dead in its tracks. If Matt here ever gets tired of the zoo world, bring him onto the team over here. Not many people can shoot like this man."

Reddman looked at the two men. "Funny, I didn't think the two of you would get on so well given your recent history together."

"That's all in the past," Malan assured him. "We actually have more in common than you might think."

Reddman looked at the horns again. "Must have been a big animal to have horns this size. Jannie, what do think? Will we get a good price for these?"

Jannie walked over and picked up the larger of the two horns. "Ja. This was from a monster. We will get top money for this."

Matt glanced over at Malan. Malan gave a brief nod, his face expressionless, hard.

I've made a deal with the devil, Matt thought, *but I have made a deal.* He would leave Malan out of any information he provided to the police or to Silke and leave the man's fate in his own hands for the time being. *But who knows what the future will hold?*

Chapter 23

While the men were in Maputaland, Cecile and her father discussed what to do.

"I should have figured it out earlier," Cecile said. "I know Afrikaans. Ontstaan means inception."

"And another word for inception is Genesis," Samuel finished. "We were worried that Jannie and Steven might be mixed up with Jonathan Tuhadeli and the land development scheme. But Steven doesn't work for Tuhadeli. Tuhadeli works for Steven."

"Genesis isn't in danger of being tainted by Ontstaan," Cecile agreed. "Genesis owns Ontstaan,"

Any doubts Cecile might have had about leaving Steven had vanished as it had become more apparent what he and Jannie had been doing through Genesis and Ontstaan Properties. It had all been there on Jannie's computer—corrupt property deals, illegal rhino horn purchases, shipments of rhino horn to Asia and the whole operation financed by a series of Chinese banks. All the dinners in San Diego and Steven's trips to Vietnam, Thailand and China were starting to make sense. *How has it come to this*? she wondered.

"The most disappointing thing is that Jannie was

complicit in all of this," Cecile said. "It will be difficult to help him if this becomes public knowledge."

"He has made his choices," Samuel said. The disappointment in his voice ran deep. Cecile knew her father to be a man of honor with a deep sense of right and wrong. To see his only son involved in such widespread criminal activity had taken a toll on him over the last week, and he seemed tired. He'd spent less time in the garden over the last three days than at any time Cecile could remember.

"If we turn this information over, we won't be able to protect Jannie," Cecile continued. "He's been far too deeply involved in this."

"I'm not sure if it will make a difference," Samuel answered. "If the newspapers and the authorities are already looking into the land deals, it may just be a matter of time before they start to unearth what is going on, with or without our help. We can support Jannie after this comes out, but one way or another, something this rotten will surface, and a price will have to be paid. I'm just glad the original homestead is still in my name and the title was never transferred to the business."

Cecile sighed. "You're right. It's not a question of hiding the information anymore. It's now a question of figuring out how to pick up the pieces once Genesis starts to come apart. I just don't like the idea of Jannie serving time in a prison."

Cecile especially feared the trauma that a public trial would cause her father. "How could I have been so foolish all these years? How could I have not seen what Steven was up to?" Her expression hardened. "I've hidden from the reality of my life for long enough. It's time to take responsibility and deal with the consequences as best we can."

* * *

Cecile sat on the sofa in the living room and leafed through an old family photo album. Seeing pictures of her mother and father together and happy brought a smile to her face. It had been too long since she'd looked at these photos, she realized. Her mother's face smiled back at her from one photo after another. *Why has that kind of happiness escaped me?* she wondered. *Was it the lack of children, or something deeper?*

She picked up her cup of tea and took a sip as she flipped another page. The album was a welcome distraction. It was Matt's final day in Kwa-Zulu Natal, and he would be leaving in the next hour to catch his flight back to the States. It was something she didn't want to think about. He had only been in the country for two weeks, but she was comfortable with the idea of him being around. His being in the house was also a convenient excuse for her to avoid talking to Steven about leaving him. Her father was right, she knew; he would not take it well.

She ran her fingers over a picture of the whole family. Her father stood with his arm wrapped around her mother's waist. Both were smiling. She was standing next to her parents looking up at them while Jannie was pulling a face for the camera. It was an old photo, but the memory seemed more recent. *What has happened to our family?*

She stood up, still holding her cup of tea, and looked out the window. Her father was there with the car, helping to put Matt's bags into the trunk. He was saying something to Matt, who just nodded his head. The two of them started to walk back to the house. Over the last couple of days, finding time to spend with Matt alone had proven difficult.

She had yearned for him to hold her, for them to have a quiet talk, but Steven had always been there, discussing Genesis and his plans for the future. Matt had been polite, professional even, but Cecile had sensed a certain hardness, a detachment, when he had talked with her husband. Steven had told her when they had returned from Maputaland that Matt would be coming to work for Genesis. He would have to wrap some things up at the National Zoo in the coming months, but then he would be taking over the North American operations of the company.

Samuel walked into the room, followed by Matt. "There you are, my dear," he said. "We've just been packing the car."

"I saw you through the window, Father. You really shouldn't be trying to pick up Matt's heavy backpack, you know," Cecile scolded him.

"You always do go on." He smiled at his daughter. "Anyway, I will leave you two alone for a few minutes. I think you both have a bit to chat about."

"Thank you, Father," Cecile said.

"I'll see you when you leave, young man," Samuel said to Matt. He then turned around and walked out the door and into the garden.

"Your father is a remarkable man," Matt said and stepped towards her.

"Yes, he is," she said as she put her arms around Matt's neck and gave him a gentle kiss on the lips. "Sit down, darling. We need to talk before you go."

"Yes, I believe we do," Matt agreed. They sat down next to each other on a couch.

Cecile stared at him for a long moment. *It is strange,* she thought. *After only two weeks, I have a deeper level of trust with this man than I have with Steven after years of marriage. I wonder if he feels the same.* But she did not say that. Instead, she asked, "When is your flight?"

"Not for a few hours. The flight back to the States actually isn't for another two days. I'm traveling down to Craddock in the Eastern Cape for a day and then on to Cape Town from where I will fly home."

"What's in Craddock?

Matt hesitated. "Cape mountain zebra are in Craddock," he replied. "I've told Steven that I am going there to visit Cape Mountain Zebra National Park. The National Zoo is looking to exhibit more zebra in the next year or two. For years we have had Grevy's zebra, but since their population has stabilized and even grown in the last few years, we'd like to focus on a more endangered subspecies of zebra. The Cape mountain zebra is at the top of the list. From Genesis's perspective, it would also be an easy animal to incorporate into the frozen zoo model."

Cecile looked at Matt. "Come on, now. That sounds like a plausible cover story for Steven, but what is the real reason you're going to Craddock? It is a dusty little town in the middle of nowhere."

Matt smiled. "It is mildly annoying that you can see through me so easily. In my defense, I did say that was what I told Steven." He paused and took a deep breath. "I'm meeting a reporter from the *Herald* there."

"And why are you doing that? This is the first chance I've had to sit down with you alone since you went to Maputaland."

"Where is Steven, by the way?" Matt asked.

"He has locked himself in his office upstairs. He asked me to come and get him when you are ready to leave. Don't worry. When he locks the office door, it takes a great deal of effort to get him back out again."

"I met the reporter in Namibia. She has been investigating poaching and the illegal rhino horn trade, and she asked me to come here to investigate Genesis." Matt took a deep breath. "The bottom line is that when she publishes her story, Steven is likely going to be arrested. Genesis is deeply involved in the illegal rhino trade and a lot more. Through a subsidiary called Ontstaan Properties, Genesis has developed a virtual monopoly over the captive rhino herds in southern Africa. Steven told me all about it when we were in Maputaland and he made his recruitment offer. He even required that I take a rhino and bring him the horns before he'd allow me into the company."

Matt looked deeply into Cecile's eyes for a long moment. "You know what he has been up to, don't you?" he said.

Cecile nodded. "Yes, but I only found out in the past couple of weeks. I had no clue before that, I swear." She frowned. "You didn't actually shoot a rhino, did you, Matt?"

"I would have if I had had to, but circumstances provided me with an easier option. Steven got his horn, but no, I didn't shoot any rhino."

"Thank God, Matt. I wouldn't want you having to do something like that for Steven's sake."

"Don't worry about me. I've done some things I'm not particularly proud of over the years. And one way or another, I knew I was going to get my hands dirty. In truth, they are already pretty filthy."

Cecile reached out her hand and placed it on Matt's knee. "I'm sorry you've been drawn into this. You're a good man, Matt Harkes, and I wouldn't want this business to hurt you in any way."

Matt smiled at Cecile and took her hand in his, squeezing it gently. "Are you and your father going to be alright when all this breaks? It could get pretty nasty, you know."

"Yes, I think so. We've had a long talk about what to do, and we both agree that whatever the truth is, however ugly it may be, we need to face it and move on from there." Cecile took her hand away from Matt's and wiped a tear away. "I've been so foolish over the years. It should never have gotten to this point."

"Yes, I talked with your dad just now. He didn't give me any details, but he told me that you've decided to help unearth what has been happening with Genesis."

Cecile nodded her head in agreement and wiped another tear away. "Look at me. I haven't cried about anything in years. I'm making a fool of myself."

"Not at all. You're being very courageous actually. Most people would be in denial about something like this, perhaps even want to cover it up and reap the benefits. You and your father are taking a very brave step, even more so because you are aware of what the consequences might be for your family."

"About Jannie," Cecile said. "I want you to know he's not a bad man. He's just done some bad things. What he has done has really hurt my father. My father doesn't show it, but he has been cut very deeply by this."

"I wish there was something I could do about that, but he is so closely tied to Steven, it is hard to see how he hasn't been stained by the whole operation."

Cecile took his hand again. She had stopped crying now and smiled at Matt. "I've got something for you," she said, reaching into her pocket and pulling out a memory stick. "I've copied all the files from Jannie's computer dealing with Genesis and Ontstaan. It's got everything you and your reporter will need to blow the lid off everything and publish the story. It will mean the end of Genesis."

Matt took the memory stick and put it into his pocket. "Thank you. I know how much this is costing you and your father."

"I've also decided to tell Steven I will be staying here and not returning to America. Our marriage has been over for some time really, and Father is going to need me around as a support in the coming weeks and months, I fear. This is my home, and it is time I returned to stay, whatever the future might hold."

"You know where to reach me if you need anything," Matt said.

Cecile nodded her head again. "Perhaps when this has all blown over, you will think to visit us again. You will always be welcome here, Matt."

They both stood up and walked to the living room door. Matt turned to face her, and Cecile put her arms around his neck, tilting her head up toward him. He put his arms around her waist, and they kissed deeply. She then nestled her head in the nape of his neck and hugged him tightly.

"I might just take you up on that invitation," he whispered into her ear.

"I hope you do," Cecile said, pulling back. "I think it is time we got you on the road."

"Yes, it is," Matt agreed.

"I'll pop upstairs and get Steven. I'll see you at the car."

* * *

"Ready for the Eastern Cape?" Reddman asked, smiling as Matt walked to the car.

"Yes, I'm looking forward to seeing the Cape Mountain Zebra National Park."

"Well, just be prepared. It's a small park compared to some of the others. More an old farm than a real park, though they do have some nice facilities."

"Yeah, that's what I've heard. But they have done a remarkable job with the Cape zebras, so it should be interesting to see." Matt put his hand into his pocket to touch the memory stick Cecile had just given him. He knew it was there, but he checked anyway. *You don't know it yet, but you and Genesis are finished,* he thought as he ran his fingers over its smooth surface. "The species may well hold opportunities for both Genesis and the National Zoo."

"Perhaps," Reddman said. "Have you seen Cecile?"

"Yes, I think she just went up to your office to look for you," Matt said. He searched Reddman's face for any clue that he was aware of what was happening between him and his wife, but saw nothing.

Reddman smiled at Matt. "I wrapped up what I was doing a bit earlier than I thought, so I came down to get some fresh air before bidding you a safe journey. I'll be in touch once you get back to the States."

"There you are, Steven. I thought you were upstairs," Cecile said as she walked out the front door.

They said their goodbyes, and Jannie got into the car with Matt to drive him to the airport.

Chapter 24

Reddman was sitting in his office at the ranch in Kwa-Zulu Natal. He was scheduled to fly back to San Diego at the end of the week. Two days had passed since Matt had left the ranch. Matt, he knew, would be flying back to the States later that day from Cape Town and could be dealt with at a later date. Cecile was more pressing. The family had been very useful to him for their land, their access to rhinos and their contacts with the power structures of the ANC. But for how much longer would he need them? The Bezuindenhouts were becoming increasingly superfluous.

Reddman thought back to that moment two days earlier when he had looked through the window and seen Matt and Cecile kissing in the living room. The initial shock had frozen him for a moment, but he had managed to pull himself together by the time Matt had come out of the house to leave.

Reddman's anger had been growing over the past two days, and he was finding it increasingly difficult to control it. He was used to being in control, and Cecile's betrayal had caught him off guard. The thought that she had been with Matt while he had been away for a couple of days in Namibia was eating at him, a growing cancer that was dominating his day. *You bitch*, he thought. *Nobody crosses me like that and gets away with it. You are mine, and you always will be.*

Edward's skull stared back at him from the desk. Reddman had a hunting knife in his hand, and he was running the tip of it around the edges of the skull's eye sockets. His mind drifted back to that night in San Diego when he had opened the package on his desk, reached in through the packing material and picked out the first of the two skulls. It had been perfectly intact, the skull of the young African-American man who had slaughtered the rhino and killed the vet. He had looked it over inch by inch and recognized with satisfaction that the Vietnamese had handled it carefully. Then he had reached in and gently lifted out the second skull. Like the one before, it had been in pristine condition, except for a small hole towards the back of the head, a bullet hole, and a larger, jagged crater in the forehead where the bullet had exited. It was the skull of the Baltimore Zoo vet. Reddman had taken a deep, slow breath and closed his eyes. He had run his fingers around the bullet hole. That hole still fascinated him, and he had let his fingers trace over it again and again every time he looked at it. It was almost perfectly round, perfectly symmetrical. Death, he knew, was a beautiful thing. Other people lived their lives afraid of it, but he knew death was something clean, something pure, something to be cherished. He thought about the woman's life, about how easily she'd been bought. All it had taken was a large sum of money, and she'd been willing to abandon her life's work of looking after animals. He thought about the years of training she had put herself through, the dedication to study and then to her job—all of it washed away because of greed. No, death wasn't ugly. It was life that was ugly. "I did you a favor," he had said as he had caressed her skull.

And now he had a third skull. It would be a wonderful addition to his collection, a collection he planned on expanding in the months and years to come.

As Reddman sat at his desk in Kwa-Zulu Natal and ran the tip of the hunting knife around the edges of the skull's eye sockets, he thought again of Cecile and her family. *She is going to pay a price for this,* he said to himself as he pressed the knife gently into the eye socket and made a movement as if he was removing an eye. *She is going to suffer.*

Cecile's father, Dr. Samuel, would go first, he decided. He was old, and there would be a number of ways to kill him. *To kill him*—the thought sent a spasm of pleasure through his body, and he shivered. *To kill him and take his head.* Then he thought of the skull he didn't have, the skull of the Vietnamese shopkeeper he had bludgeoned to death outside Saigon. It had been too many years since he'd killed. The Namibian head, he decided, would be the last trophy he collected from someone he didn't kill himself. *Soon I will start collecting my own heads.*

He stood up and walked to the office window. It overlooked the swimming pool and the back garden stretching beyond. Cecile's father was tending his flower beds with Boysen close by. It looked like they were arguing again. *Silly old fool. You'll be dead soon, so enjoy your flowers while you can.*

I'm so tired of this family, Reddman said to himself. *And I don't need them anymore.* His course of action was already decided, though he still needed to plan out the details. He would kill the whole family. Cecile's father would be first, then Cecile once she returned to America with him and finally Jannie at some date in the future. He again looked down on Samuel. Cecile's father was bent over, weeding between the flowers now. He looked frail and weak, more frail and weak than previously. *Your age is finally starting to weigh on you. You will be easy to kill.*

He thought about what he'd need to do to kill Samuel. He would need to get him alone, to isolate him away from the other members of the family and the staff at the ranch. The timing would have to be thought out as well. He would need to do it in such a way that no suspicion would fall on him.

Reddman smiled for the first time in two days. Cecile's betrayal had freed him, he realized. Now there was nothing to stop him from killing them all. He just needed to take his time and plan things carefully. A triple murder with no suspicion falling on him—it would be a challenge, but one that could be overcome. *Be patient, that's the key. Take your time and think it through.*

How will I collect their heads? The thought occurred to him, and he smiled again. *That will be another challenge, claiming their heads for my collection without casting any suspicion on myself.*

"Steven, are you in there?"

It was Cecile, knocking on the office door.

Steven picked up the skull from the desk and put it in one of the lower drawers. "Yes, I am. I'm just wrapping up some work. Is there something you need?"

"Yes, we need to have a chat. There's something I need to tell you."

"I'll be down in a few minutes. I'll see you in the living room."

Reddman leaned back in his chair, the knife still in his hands. He rotated the handle, watching the sunlight reflect off the stainless steel blade. After a few moments, he stood up. Putting the blade back into its sheath, he slipped it into his back pocket. What on earth could the bitch want to talk about? *Probably wants another shopping trip into Durban.*

*   *   *

Cecile was sitting on the couch near the window when Reddman walked into the room.

Reddman sat in one of the easy chairs and looked at his wife. "What's on your mind?" he said. "I suppose you want to head into town again for some more shopping."

"You don't have to take that tone with me," Cecile said. "And quite frankly, no, it has nothing to do with that."

"Well, then, what is so important that you would come upstairs banging on my office door and interrupting my work?"

Cecile glared at him a moment and paused to collect herself. It had been a long time since she had stood up to Steven, but she was now ready to deal with the truth about their relationship. In the days when Steven had been away and she had been with Matt, she knew she had crossed a threshold, and now there was no stepping back. Her research into what Steven and Jannie had been doing had only confirmed her decision. She didn't know when the story about Genesis and Ontstaan Properties would break in the news, but she knew it was coming, and she wanted to have made the break with Steven by then.

"Well, then, cat got your tongue?" Reddman continued.

"No, not at all," Cecile said. "I won't be coming back to San Diego with you later this week." It was said. Cecile felt a brief moment of relief, as if a weight had been lifted.

"What do you mean you won't be coming back with me? Our time here on this trip is over, and I've got to get back to deal with some important business."

"I don't think you heard me, Steven. I didn't say you won't be going back to San Diego. I said I won't be going with you."

"What are you saying?" Steven said, his face turning red with anger. "You will be coming back with me."

"No. No, I won't," Cecile said. She had seen Steven get angry before and had always shied away from his aggression, but it was different this time. She stood up and faced him.

"I'm leaving you, Steven. I will not be returning to San Diego with you this week or at any time in the future."

Reddman, still seated, glared back at her. "You whore! I go away for a few days, and you start a relationship behind my back with a business associate. And now you think you can just leave me?"

Cecile, surprised that he knew about Matt, stared open-mouthed at her husband.

"That's right. I saw you kissing him that last day through the living room window."

"What happened with Matt has nothing to do with this. It has been coming for a long time. I've finally opened my eyes and seen you for who you really are."

Reddman stood up, took a step towards Cecile and slapped her powerfully across the side of the head. She stumbled sideways and fell back onto the sofa.

"Who are you kidding? You have no idea who I really am, bitch."

Reddman stepped forward to hit her again.

"Step away from my daughter. You will not touch her again."

Reddman turned to see Samuel enter the room. Reddman took a step back from Cecile as Samuel strode over and stood between Reddman and his daughter.

"Are you alright, my dear?" Samuel asked, not taking his eyes off Reddman. "What the hell do you think…"

He didn't get the chance to finish his sentence as Reddman's fist crashed into his face, sending him sprawling backwards onto the floor, blood flowing from his nose.

"You stupid, old man! Never come between me and my wife again!" Reddman snarled.

"What are you doing?" Cecile got up and went over to her prone father. "Have you lost your mind? You could have killed him."

She knelt down and checked his breathing. It was steady, but his eyes were closed, and blood was running from his broken nose down the side of his cheek.

"Get out of this house now," Cecile said as she started to get up. She glared at Reddman as he reached into his back pocket and pulled out his knife. She looked at his face then, and for the first time she saw the madness in his eyes. "Stay away from us!" she screamed at him as he stepped towards them. Cecile bent over her father to protect him from the blow that she saw coming.

"What's happening in here?" Jannie said as he entered the room. "You're making such a racket people can hear you all the way out in the bush."

He was looking at Reddman's back and his sister bent over his prone father. "Is he alright?" he asked and stepped quickly across the room toward Samuel.

As he walked by Reddman, Steven turned towards him. Jannie saw the flash of the blade, but he was too close to Reddman to react. His brother-in-law plunged the knife into his stomach and wrapped an arm around his neck, drawing him more deeply onto the blade. Jannie gasped in pain and surprise. Reddman twisted the blade as he held Jannie up.

"Your sister and your father will be next, you stupid Boer," Reddman said. He pulled the blade out slowly and then plunged it back into Jannie's stomach.

Jannie gave him a confused look and, with the last of his strength, pushed himself free. He staggered back, holding his hand over his stomach. "Why?" he spat out, blood dribbling from the corner of his mouth, as his legs gave out and he collapsed backwards to the floor. He turned his head towards his sister as he died, his last sight the horrified look on her face.

Reddman stood over Jannie for a moment. Then a wave of exhilaration seemed to sweep over him, and he started to laugh.

"You've killed him," Cecile sobbed as she cradled her father, but Reddman did not appear to have heard.

Reddman looked down at the knife in his hand, the blade still covered in Jannie's blood. He looked again at Jannie, whose lifeless body lay sprawled across the carpeting in front of him. "You're mine now," he said as he stepped towards the body and knelt down. He pulled Jannie's collar away from his neck and then took hold of his hair to keep his head still as he cut. He smiled as he pressed the knife into Jannie's neck. The blade was sharp, but not long enough. It kept getting stuck as he sawed it backward and forward. Blood poured easily onto the floor, soaking the carpet a deep red.

"Get away from him!" Cecile cried as she kicked out at Reddman's head. He saw the kick coming out of the side of his eye and moved his head just in time. Her foot caught him a glancing blow to the head and knocked him off balance for a moment. For the first time, Cecile saw the deep gash in her brother's neck and gasped, horrified at what she saw. "You're insane!" she cried out and, choking back a sob, tried to kick him again.

Her pause to look at her brother had given Reddman the moment he needed. "Your turn, bitch," he said as he dodged her next kick easily and got back to his feet.

Cecile saw the animal look in his eye and took a step backwards. "Get away from us!" she sobbed as Reddman took a step forward and slashed at her with the knife. She raised her right arm to protect herself and took the blow on her forearm. The knife bit deeply into the muscle, and she fell backwards, tumbling against one of the chairs.

"You're all pathetic." Reddman laughed. "Say hello to your brother when you see him."

Reddman stepped forward, his large body looming over her as grinned down at her. "You were never going to leave me. You were a fool to think I would ever let that happen."

Cecile felt the warm blood running down her arm, but raised it again to protect herself.

"Pathetic," Reddman said as he drew the knife back to slash her again.

A gunshot exploded behind him, and a bullet tore past the left side of his head, ripping off the top half of his ear. He stumbled over Cecile's legs and tripped to his knees. The knife bounced across the floor as he tried to catch himself. It took him a moment to regain his bearings, and in that time, Cecile had crawled away, back towards her father. Reddman looked back at the door. Boysen stood there with one of Jannie's hunting rifles pointed at his head.

Reddman reached up and lightly touched the side of his head. The blood from his ear was running freely down the side of his neck. He glared at Boysen and screamed, "They are mine!"

Boysen, looking calmly down the sights of the gun, replied, "No, Mr. Reddman, they are not yours. You will go now, or my next shot will not just remove the ear from the side of your head." He glanced at Cecile and her father and then at Jannie's body. "I should kill you now," he said. "But there has been enough violence here today, and I don't want your blood on my hands. I will let the police take care of you."

Reddman screamed in rage and frustration as he looked at Jannie's body and then back at Cecile and her father, "They are mine!"

"Go now or die now. The choice is yours."

Boysen held the rifle steady and did not blink. As the gardener circled the room, Reddman backed out the door and then ran, not stopping until he got into one of the cars and drove off the farm.

Chapter 25

The sound of distant thunder rolled over the zoo grounds. Matt looked to the sky one last time before he went back inside the rhino building. The air was thick and moist, and a line of black clouds towered over the horizon to the west, promising high winds and heavy rain.

Another late afternoon thunderstorm, Matt thought and smiled. He enjoyed summer thunderstorms even if they involved a bit of extra work to make sure the animals were all settled in for the night. The forecast was for the storm to be particularly strong as a cold front was poised to push across the East Coast later that evening. Matt had just completed his rounds of the zoo, making sure all the animals in his care were inside, out of harm's way. For once, the sounds of the city that surrounded the zoo seemed to have grown silent as the storm gathered its strength and drew closer.

It was late in the day, and the zoo gates were closed to the public. Most of the staff had already gone home after finishing their daily routines. Matt enjoyed the zoo at this time of day. He could walk alone along the tree-lined pathways that snaked around the zoo grounds with no crowds to distract him from his thoughts. His nightly routine always ended at the rhino building in which his small office was located. This night, a stack of paperwork sat on his desk detailing a breeding recommendation for one of the white rhinos in his care. The animal, a cantankerous male, was to be sent to a facility in Florida in the coming weeks.

Might as well get started, he thought. *It will just be there in the morning if I don't get it done now.* Reviewing such paperwork was tedious, but it was better to do it when he wasn't distracted. His office, for what it was worth, was a desk with a computer tucked into the far corner of the building. Not that he minded. He enjoyed having the animals close by him. All of their sounds and smells were part of what made working at a zoo special.

Matt walked by the enclosure of the large, male white rhino, which was eating hay. Matt stopped for a moment to watch the animal eat.

"How are you, bud?" he asked. "You don't know all the trouble you've caused, do you? Don't worry about it, though. You'll be going on vacation soon enough."

The rhino flicked its ears towards the sound of Matt's voice, stared myopically in his direction and then put its head back down to take another mouthful of hay.

Matt smiled at the great animal. "I expect you'll have more luck with the ladies in Florida than I've had lately."

He'd been back in the States for four months with no word from Suzanne. He had called three times and sent her a couple of e-mails once he was settled back in after his second Africa trip, but he had heard nothing back from her. Her silence hurt, but he knew there was little else he could do now. If she was to come back, it would be on her own terms and in her own time. So he let it rest and tried to push her to the back of his mind.

Maybe I'll visit her folks this weekend, check in on them and see how she is doing, he thought.

Cecile had called the previous month to check in with him.

"Dad is doing alright, though he seems very tired these days. Jannie's death has really taken a lot out of him," she had said. She had sounded tired herself. Matt had been following the story in the news, and despite the media coverage and intense police search, there had been no sign of Reddman. The police had found the farm vehicle in which he had fled in an abandoned lot in Durban's commercial district. The vehicle had been torched, and there were no clues to Reddman's whereabouts.

"I'm so sorry about Jannie. I know you loved him very much," Matt had said. Cecile had taken a moment to answer. "You're not crying, are you?" he had asked. "I didn't mean to upset you."

"It's alright. I just struggle when I think what Steven did to Jannie, what he was going to do to my father and me if Boysen hadn't shown up," Cecile had said. "Did you hear what the police found in our San Diego home, in his office? How could I have been so blind to what he was, to who he was?"

Matt had known that she was talking about the two skulls. The police had searched Reddman's San Diego home in the week after he had killed Jannie and then vanished. They had discovered the skulls, and subsequent tests had showed them to be from the Maryland vet and a young African-American male from Baltimore. The South African police had also found Edward's skull in Reddman's office at the ranch in Kwa-Zulu Natal. But with Reddman missing, Malan somewhere in Maputaland and Jannie dead, no one knew where the skull had come from. No one but Matt, and again he remained silent on the matter. *Best to let sleeping dogs lie,* he thought. *And the man deserved what he got for what he was going to do to Silke.*

"Steven was a manipulative man who fooled a lot of good people for a long time, myself included," Matt had said. "From what I understand, you did all you could to help your father. And don't worry too much about Steven. He's not likely to drop off the police's radar screen, either here or in South Africa. As soon as he shows his face, he will be picked up right away." Matt had said it to reassure Cecile, but he wasn't so confident himself.

How could a man who was international news and wanted in South Africa and America for murder vanish so quickly and for so long? Matt wondered as he looked at the rhino eating. He knew the answer, though. *Money. It all comes down to money in the end.*

He turned away from the rhino and walked over to the desk. He pulled out the chair and sat down, turning on the monitor to his computer as he did so. He wanted to go online and check the weather one last time before the storm hit. These summer thunderstorms could be powerful, but they didn't usually last long.

The stack of paperwork sat next to his monitor. *I'll get to that as soon I've checked the weather,* he promised himself.

A clap of thunder enveloped the building, and Matt felt a warm, humid gust of air brush against the back of his neck. "Blasted door," he said to himself as he got up to close it.

As he turned away from his desk, he saw a figure standing by the open door.

"Hello, Matt," the man said.

Matt knew instantly who it was. Steven Reddman stood

in front of him wearing blue jeans and a light jacket. His sharp blue eyes glared at Matt before he swung the door shut behind him and turned the dead bolt. His hair was still cropped close, and Matt could see where the bullet had torn away the top half of his ear. The flesh was pink, but it had healed. It gave him a slightly grotesque look.

"I wouldn't want anybody to interrupt our reunion," Reddman said as the dead bolt slid into place. His voice was flat, but Matt could see he was struggling to control himself as he slowly reached into his coat and pulled out a machete.

Matt froze. There was no way out of the building but through the door that Reddman had just closed. There was no time to call for help. Reddman swung the machete in front of his body.

"So, how was my wife when you last saw her?" he growled at Matt. "You think I would let you get away with sleeping with her? She was mine...is mine...and nobody and nothing will ever change that."

Matt took a deep breath to slow his own breathing. He glanced quickly around and realized there was nothing within reach that he would be able to use to defend himself. *Stay calm, be quick*, he thought. Reddman stepped closer as Matt eyed him warily. He was a big man, but he looked older than Matt remembered. Matt looked at the machete as Reddman swung it in front of himself again. *He's old and slow*, Matt thought. *The only problem is the machete.*

"She was never really yours anyway," Matt said. "And I didn't take her. You lost her long before I came along." *Goad him. Let his anger take over, and he'll make a mistake.*

"You lie!" Reddman shouted, his face contorting in anger.

"You're a pathetic man. She knew it, I know it, and now, thanks to your own stupidity, the whole world knows it." Matt snapped at him. *The angrier I get him, the less careful he'll be when he comes at me.*

"You are going to pay for that!" Reddman screamed, and Matt sensed he was about to attack.

"What are you here for anyway? You vanished, got away. No one was going to find you," Matt continued.

"I'm here for your head," Reddman spat out as he lunged at Matt, swinging the machete towards Matt's head and neck. He moved surprisingly quickly but still was not fast enough, as Matt ducked under the blow and stepped past him. As he did so, he unleashed a vicious punch that caught Reddman in the stomach. Reddman grunted but otherwise didn't seem hurt. He turned quickly to again face Matt, who now had his back to the rhino enclosure.

Matt eyed the older man closely. The punch he had landed would have floored many men, but not Reddman.

"I can do this all night," Reddman said with a sneer.

"We will see about that," Matt replied. *He's old,* Matt reminded himself. *Tough but old. He will tire quickly.*

Reddman feigned another lunge, but Matt only took a step back. Matt sensed he was getting close to the enclosure, and out of the corner of his eye he saw the large, male rhino chewing on its hay.

"Did you really think you'd be able to get away with a scheme like that?" Matt asked as Reddman took another step forward. "You were bound to be exposed sometime."

"You're a fool, Harkes. We could have saved the rhino and made a fortune at the same time. Now, instead of that, you are going to die tonight."

He swung the machete again, this time in a downward

stroke. Matt dodged to the side as the blade slashed against the steel bars of the rhino enclosure. The rhino glared in the direction of the sound and snorted.

"You're getting old and slow," Matt taunted.

Reddman swung the machete another time, again missing. Matt noticed Reddman was getting flushed, and his breathing was becoming labored.

"Tired, old man? I thought you said you could do this all night," Matt taunted. He wanted to draw Reddman in. He had noticed that every time Reddman attacked, he led with the same leg, planting it out well in front of his body.

Reddman drew the machete back and took a step towards Matt. This time Matt didn't wait for the blow to be delivered. He stepped forward himself and drove the underside of his right foot into Reddman's knee. Matt threw all his weight into the blow, and Reddman's knee bent backwards and snapped. The machete fell out of his hands as he clasped his leg and fell to the ground, screaming in agony. Matt quickly kicked the machete out of Reddman's reach.

Matt went back to the desk and caught his breath. He looked back at Reddman. The man was lying prone on the ground with both hands wrapped around his shattered knee. The lower part of his leg was bent forward at an awkward angle.

"This isn't over yet," Reddman gasped through the pain.

"Yes, it is," Matt replied. "I'll call the police in a minute. Then you will be going away for the rest of your life."

"You're a fool, Harkes. Even from prison, I'll be able to reach out for you and Cecile. My Vietnamese friends will be only too happy to go after you both for the trouble you've caused. Money is a powerful incentive. One word from me, and you'll never live in peace."

"You're lying. If that were the case, you would have sent them this time."

Reddman lifted his head to stare at Matt. "You are wrong there, Harkes. I wanted the pleasure of killing you myself and starting a new collection with your head. Cecile would have followed you to your grave soon after. You may have won tonight, but only for tonight. Both you and that whore will die before too long."

Reddman crawled towards the rhino enclosure and pulled himself up, using the bars.

"You see, there is no way you can win," Reddman said and laughed. "You are going to die, and then Cecile and her father. They won't be easy deaths either."

Matt stood up and walked towards Reddman. Matt could see that Reddman had gone over the edge now, a madness sweeping away what sanity he had left. *This ends now,* he thought.

"Call the police? What are you going to do?" Reddman laughed.

Matt's fist cut the laugh short as it crashed into Reddman's jaw. Reddman collapsed to the ground again, but continued to laugh.

"You are going to die, Harkes, and there is nothing you can do to stop it."

Matt stood over the broken man and stared down at him. A wave of anger crashed over him, and thoughts raced through his head. *All the people who have died because of your greed. All the animals that have been killed because you wanted money. All the pain and anguish you've caused for the sake of killing rhino. You are wrong. I can stop it.*

"It ends here tonight," Matt said. He felt strangely calm, having said it. He knew what he was going to do, and there would be no feelings of guilt after it was done.

"No, it doesn't!" Reddman shrieked hysterically, spit frothing from between his lips. "Haven't you been listening to me?"

Matt reached down and grabbed Reddman by his collar, dragging him across the floor. Reddman cried out in pain as his shattered leg slid across the concrete.

"You're not going to kill me, are you?" Reddman babbled.

"I've killed one man because of you, and I won't do it again. But you will die tonight. Of that I am certain."

Still holding Reddman's collar, Matt unlocked the gate to the rhino enclosure and opened it. He pulled Reddman inside, dropping him onto the floor.

Reddman looked around and started to get his bearings. "What are you doing? You can't leave me in here!" he shrieked as Matt walked out and closed and locked the gate behind him.

"I would be quiet if I were you. You don't want to get that fellow's attention," Matt said, pointing to the male rhino that was now looking in Reddman's direction, flicking its ears at the sound of his voice.

"Let me out," Reddman pleaded, dragging himself to the side of the enclosure.

"I don't think I will," Matt said walking over to his computer and turning it off. He then picked up the machete using a handkerchief and looked around the building. There were no signs of the struggle that had just taken place.

Reddman, now standing on one leg, looked at the machete and stuck his arm through the bars, "Give it to me. I might stand a chance with it."

Matt looked at the blade and then at Reddman. "This wouldn't do you much good, and I don't want you hurting him," he said pointing to the rhino. "He's got to go to Florida on a breeding loan in a few weeks. My guess is that, if you are very quiet and stay very still, you might last an hour with this guy. But I wouldn't bet on it. He has a nasty temper with strangers in his enclosure."

Matt smiled grimly. He would give Reddman back the machete after all, he decided. But not until the morning, when he could place it next to Reddman's mangled body after he had unlocked the enclosure gate. Clearly, the man was crazy, and it would be in keeping with his character that he would go into the pen with a machete to obtain one more set of horns. Matt put the machete down carefully under the desk, out of sight. For now, he desperately needed to be with someone. It didn't really matter who, as long as there was someone to corroborate that he was not here, with Reddman.

With that, Matt turned away, walked to the door, unlocked the dead bolt and opened it. A clap of thunder sounded, and warm, heavy raindrops hit his face. He turned the lights off, closed the door and walked into the storm.

*　*　*

Reddman stood still on his one good leg in the dark, one arm holding onto a steel bar for support. His eyes had adjusted to the lack of light, but he still was having a hard time seeing the rhino. He could hear its breathing, broken by the occasional powerful snort. He pressed himself as tightly as he could to the steel bars and tried to keep himself as still as possible. A vague, gray shape loomed out of the darkness, and Reddman felt the warm flow of his own urine run down the inside of his legs as he closed his eyes.

The great horn took him just below the ribs, driving straight through his body and breaking his spine. The rhino backed away, shaking its head to dislodge Reddman, who then slumped to the ground. Reddman opened his eyes but couldn't focus on anything. The taste of blood filled his mouth. *Where is the rhino?* he wondered as he lay there, soaked in his own blood and urine. A few minutes passed. *Maybe it is going to leave me alone now,* he thought. *Maybe there is still a chance I will live through this.*

Then he felt it. A great pressure building on the side of his head as the rhino drove down its wide foot. The pressure and pain grew, and Reddman started to scream. No sound came out of his mouth as his skull cracked and his head exploded.

www.ingramcontent.com/pod-product-compliance
Lightning Source LLC
Chambersburg PA
CBHW020057180626
46812CB00006B/2372